KIDNAPPED!

Louisa entered the storage room and went a couple of feet, stopping in consternation when she didn't see any dresses or packing crates or anything. The room contained a table and two chairs, and a cot with a rope coiled under it against the far wall. On the table were a coffee pot and two cups, as well as a deck of cards. Some of the cards were spread out, face down, as if someone had been playing a game and been interrupted. "What in the world?" She heard the door shut.

As Lou began to swivel, steely arms encircled her from behind, pinning her own. For an instant she was too startled to do anything. Then another man, a brute with a scar on his cheek, came from behind and lifted a strip of cloth toward her mouth to gag her. Galvanized by fear, Lou kicked him, catching him in the groin. The brute grunted and staggered backward. She opened her mouth to scream but the man holding her pressed a hand over her mouth.

"Please don't make a sound!"

WILDERNESS

Savages

David Thompson

LEISURE BOOKS NEW YORK CITY

To Judy, Joshua, and Shane

A LEISURE BOOK®

May 2000

Published by

Dorchester Publishing Co., Inc.
276 Fifth Avenue
New York, NY 10001

ISBN 0-8439-4711-X

Printed in the United States of America.

Savages

Chapter One

"How much farther, do you reckon?"

Zachary King rose in his stirrups to scan the prairie ahead. For what seemed ages they had been traveling steadily eastward across the vast sea of grass, and he knew his companion was eager to reach their destination. He wasn't, though. Not when there would be thousands upon thousands of whites, with nearly every one looking down their nose at him. "Another day or two," he guessed.

Louisa May Clark sniffed in irritation. She was tired of the heat, the dust, the endless hours spent in the saddle. Every morning when she woke, her legs were so sore and stiff she could hardly walk. Tilting her head back to squint at the sun, she muttered, "Well, a couple of more shouldn't kill us."

They had come close to dying several times. Once from a buffalo stampede. Once during a fierce afternoon storm when a bolt of lightning crashed to earth twenty yards from the gully they had sought shelter in. And a third time when curious wolves nearly spooked their horses into running off.

Both Zach and Lou were dressed in buckskins that clung to their youthful frames. Zach was strongly built for his age, his piercing green eyes in stark contrast to his raven-black hair, which hung in thick braids. Across his chest were slanted a powder horn, ammunition pouch, and possibles bag. On his left hip hung a Bowie, a gift from his father for his eighteenth birthday. Tucked under his wide brown leather belt, on either side of the big buckle, was a matched set of flintlock pistols. A heavy Hawken rested across his thighs.

Louisa's eyes were deepest blue, her face tanned bronze yet still a lighter shade than his. Befitting someone who had recently turned seventeen, her lovely features were taking on an air of maturity. Sandy hair cascaded well past her slender shoulders. Now, arching an eyebrow in response to his sour expression, she asked, "Having second thoughts?"

"I want you to be happy," Zach said. Which avoided the question nicely.

Smiling, Louisa leaned toward him and gave his arm a gentle squeeze. For once in her life she had done something right. She had found someone who loved her with his whole heart and soul, someone who would do anything for her. Lou couldn't wait to become his, officially. She couldn't wait for the preacher to declare, "I pronounce you husband and wife."

Zach returned her smile, but his gut tightened into a knot. He wouldn't be bound for St. Louis if not for her. In his estimation, it was unnecessary. There was no need for a formal white wedding, not when a Shoshone ceremony would suffice.

"I still can't believe they went to so much bother on my account," Lou commented, patting her possibles bag. In it was the letter she had received from her aunt, delivered by a friend of Zach's father. "And how in tarnation did my aunt track Jim Bridger down?"

"He's fairly famous, as mountaineers go," Zach mentioned. "Your aunt paid a visit to the Hawken gun shop, and he just happened to be there. She'd heard tell that's where most trappers and mountain men are outfitted for the Rockies."

"Mighty clever of her," Louisa said. She had always liked her aunt Martha, her mother's older sister. When she was a little girl, Martha used to perch her on a knee and tell her fables and stories. And later Martha had given her a doll she'd treasured until a neighbor's dog ripped it to ribbons.

"I suppose," Zach said. The way he saw it, Martha Livingston was more a meddler than anything else. He'd been all set to take Lou as his wife and had even picked out a site for their cabin when the letter came, saying how Martha and other in-laws of Lou's would be in St. Louis for the entire month of August, and requesting Zebulon and Louisa join them there. Lou's relatives had no idea that Zeb, her pa, had been killed by a war party, slain while trying to defend his hard-earned furs.

Lou recognized her betrothed's tone. "You'll enjoy meeting them. They're fine folks, all of them. As friendly as can be. Trust me."

Zach trusted her with his life. It was her relatives he was wary of, just as he was wary of every white. Half-breeds weren't held in high esteem by most, an injustice that rankled him like an open sore.

"As I recollect," Louisa chattered on, "Aunt Martha was four years older than Marcy, my mother. She's married to a lawyer by the name of Earnest. Her oldest son, my cousin Harry, also came. Then there's my uncle from my pa's side of the family, and his two daughters." Beaming, she declared, "Oh, Stalking Coyote, it will be grand to see them again!"

Zach grunted. She had used his Shoshone name, as she often did at emotional moments. He would try to like her relations, but it might prove difficult. By and large, whites held dim views of those of mixed blood.

9

Their horses, his dun and her mare, plodded wearily on until shortly past noon. Thanks to Zach's keen eyesight, he spotted a bump on the horizon long before Lou did, a bump that grew larger and larger, slowly taking on the dimensions of an isolated dwelling made mainly of sod. Zach had never seen the like. Fresh-hung laundry strung between two saplings was proof the house was occupied, as were three horses in a small corral.

"Oh, look!" Lou exclaimed. "We must be getting close to civilization."

"Wonderful."

A ten-acre plot had been tilled. Rows of corn were the result. Examining the stalks was a gangly man in overalls and a floppy hat who glanced up sharply at their approach. His mouth going slack, he spun and sped to the homestead, bawling at the top of his lungs, "Beth! Beth! Fetch my long gun! Injuns are comin'!"

A stout woman in a homespun dress and faded apron filled the doorway and handed the farmer a Kentucky rifle. He had it snug against his shoulder when Zach and Lou reined up a dozen feet out.

"Howdy, mister," Lou said amiably. "Sorry if we startled you. But as you can see, I'm not an Indian."

"Dog my cats!" the farmer blurted. "A white gal, ridin' alone with the likes of a mangy redskin." He emphasized his point by swinging the rifle's muzzle toward Zach. "What tribe are you from, Injun? You don't look like no Otoe or Pawnee I ever saw."

Lou answered before Zach could. "He's part Shoshone, and as friendly as I am. There's no need to be waving a gun at us."

"Says you, missy," the settler responded. "Not three months ago some redskins massacred a family north of here. We never did learn what kind are to blame. Not that it's important." The man glared at Zach. "In my book, all Injuns are the same. The world's better off without 'em."

"You can't mean that," Lou said. "Indians are people, just like us. There are good ones and bad ones—"

The farmer wouldn't listen. "I've yet to hear tell of an Injun worth the powder it would take to make worm food of him. Didn't Andrew Jackson, back when he was president, say we should rub out every last one? Seems to me if anyone should know what to do with 'em, it's a leader of our country."

Zach wanted to tear the gun from the man's hands and shove it down his throat. Time and again he'd run into bigots just like this settler. Men who shared the same senseless attitude, who spouted the same mindless hatred. Beckoning Louisa, he raised his reins to ride off.

"All we want to know is how far we are from St. Louis," Lou said.

"You're not thinkin' of going there with *him*?" the farmer said. "Hell, girl. They eat Injuns alive in the big city."

His wife, who had listened to the exchange as calmly as could be, abruptly tapped the farmer on the left shoulder. "Tell her, Jeb."

"Ah, Beth. They'll find out soon enough on their own. I don't much like helpin' an Injun."

"Then I'll do it," Beth said, and gestured to the southeast. "You've got about a two-day ride, dear. Just keep going east until you come to the Mississippi, and follow it south. You can't hardly miss St. Louis."

"We're grateful, ma'am," Lou said sincerely, adding, "You have my sympathy, being tied to a mule who goes through life with blinders on."

"Who are you calling a mule?" the farmer demanded, taking a step toward them.

"Behave yourself, Jeb," Beth said. "She's young. She doesn't mean any harm."

Lou flicked her reins and Zach kept pace, smoldering like an ember in a fire. It wasn't in his nature to suffer abuse meekly, as a white missionary had once told him he should do. No Shoshone warrior worthy of the name would stand for being insulted. At the very least, he should have counted coup on the farmer by bashing the fool over the head with his Henry.

11

"How could a woman marry a man like that?" Lou idly mused. Grinning at Zach, she said, "Thank goodness you're not like him. The Good Lord did me a favor by bringing the two of us together. You'll make a terrific husband, as understanding and considerate as you are."

It embarrassed Zach when she gushed like that. He had flaws, as everyone did. But there were times when he suspected she tended to turn a blind eye to them. Which might pose problems later on. As his father once advised, "See people for how they really are, son, and not as you'd like them to be. Always remember, a person is like a deck of cards. For every card they turn over, for every part of them they let you see, there are more parts they don't show anyone."

Zach had been thinking about his pa a lot in recent days. How Nate was always there when Zach needed him. How his father stood by him through thick and thin, even when he did stupid things that brought trouble down on the family. His pa was exactly the sort of father Zach wanted to be to his own children, but he wasn't sure he had it in him. He would be the first to admit he wasn't as levelheaded as he should be. Yet another problem to face in the future.

Lou looked at him, noted he was troubled, and jumped to the conclusion that their pending arrival in St. Louis was to blame. She was well aware of how uncomfortable Zach was around whites. But she believed he brought it on himself. People were a lot better than Zach gave them credit for being.

Soon they saw another homestead, then another, and before long they were following a rutted dirt track that served as a road. It passed through a thick belt of trees and brush. Presently they drew rein on the bank of the mighty Mississippi.

"Look at it!" Lou said, giddy with delight. Here was spectacular proof their long trek was honestly and truly near an end. "Isn't it amazing?"

Zach had seen it once before, as a small boy. It had impressed him then; it impressed him even more now. According to his father, the Mississippi was the largest river to be found between the Atlantic and the Pacific. Most Indian tribes gave it a name that translated as "Great River." It was said an explorer once traced the Mississippi to its source, which turned out to be a little stream about a foot and a half wide, far to the north. But Zach found that hard to accept. Especially at the moment, when before him stretched an expanse of water that must be a mile wide from shore to shore. It dwarfed the Columbia, the Wind River, the Green, and every other waterway he'd seen.

"Oh, what I wouldn't give to be able to jump in," Lou said. "It's been so long since I had a bath, I itch all over."

The current didn't appear all that swift, but Zach was glad she didn't attempt it. He'd witnessed a Shoshone maiden drown once and didn't want the same awful fate to befall Lou. For hours they paralleled the shore. Reaching the junction with the Missouri River, they had to locate a ford. They had forded the Missouri once before, far back on the prairie, but had shunned it afterward because a Sioux war party had been in the vicinity. Now, as they continued along the Mississippi, Zach noticed something strange. "Part of the river is clear and the other part is the color of blood."

"Remember how red the Missouri was?" Lou reminded him. "For miles the two somehow flow side by side without mixing. Later on the waters do mingle, and then the Mississippi looks like liquid mud. Which is why some folks call it the Big Muddy."

They rode on. Within a mile they emerged from trees and came on a cluster of dilapidated buildings, plank-and-log affairs that didn't appear strong enough to withstand a strong breeze. Four of the five were small, but at the center was a long building bearing a crudely painted sign that boasted, SLIM'S DRY GOODS, HARNESS, FOOD AND DRINK,

13

FARM TOOLS AND FRILLS FOR THE LADIES! LAST STOP BETWEEN HERE AND CALIFORNIA!

"Oh, my!" Lou's eyes sparkled. She hadn't stepped foot in a store in almost two years. Two years since she saw a real dress, two years since she held a swatch of cloth in her hands, since she fondled jewelry or sniffed the latest perfumes. "Can we stop? Please?"

Zach was uneasy. Two wagons were parked out front, and six horses lined a hitch rail. Worse, two scruffy characters in greasy clothes lounged nearby and both were regarding him with open hostility. But it was impossible for him to deny her. "Only for a little while."

Lou trotted to an empty rail and was off the mare in a bound. Gleeful as a little girl on her first shopping spree, she bounced indoors. Aisles of untidy merchandise unfolded, many of the articles layered with dust. But to her, they were treasures beyond compare.

Outside, Zach dismounted and looped the reins fast. He climbed the steps to the long porch slowly, conscious of the flinty stares of the duo. They were unkempt, their cheeks smeared with dirt. Each sported a brace of pistols and a rifle. Strolling in, he paused to let his eyes adjust to the dim light. Lou was flitting from shelf to shelf like a hummingbird from flower to flower. Beyond her were a middle-aged man and woman, farmers evidently, watching Lou in amusement. Seeing him, they both visibly stiffened and whispered to one another.

Against the far wall was a counter, and behind it a man as thin as the horse rail. Slim, Zach figured. The man nodded and smiled at him, but to Zach that meant nothing. He had learned the hard way that whites sometimes weren't as friendly as they put on. Cradling the Hawken in the crook of an arm, he ambled in his sweetheart's wake.

"Look at this!" Lou gushed. "As I live and breathe, a set of silverware! Here in the middle of nowhere! And these blankets! Feel how soft they are. And, oh, there's a rack of ready-made dresses! Come take a gander."

Zach would rather not. Sometimes Lou tended to forget he was a Shoshone warrior, and that certain pastimes were beneath a warrior's dignity. Admiring dresses was one of them. Instead, he strolled to the counter and turned so his back was against it to keep an eye on the entrance.

The proprietor sidled over. "Howdy, son. The handle is Slim. Pleased to meet you." He held out his hand.

Suspicious of a trick, Zach cautiously shook. "Zachary King."

Slim blinked, then gaped. "I'll be switched. You're part white, ain't you? I'd never have guessed."

"Something wrong with that?" Zach asked more harshly than he intended. The incident with the farmer had left him primed to explode.

"Heck, no," Slim said good-naturedly. "Some of my best customers are Indians. I don't hold anything against anyone for the color of their skin. We can't help how we're born, can we?"

"I wish more whites shared your view," Zach commented wistfully. As if on cue, two figures filled the doorway. The scruffy pair planted themselves with their arms folded across their chests and arrogantly glared at him.

"Damn," Slim said, then lowered his voice to a whisper. "Listen, friend. A word to the wise. That pair can be a heap of trouble if they're of a mind. So whatever you do, don't rile them if you can help it." He spoke faster as the duo slowly advanced. "They're part of the Hogan clan. A bunch of uppity river rats who act like they own the river. Tangle with one and you'll have the whole clan down on your head. You don't want that."

"I wasn't brought up in the woods to be scared by owls," Zach responded.

"Maybe so, but they're snake-mean. The short rooster on the left is called Rufus. The hefty one is his brother, Charlie. The last time they were here, they set a poor old Otoe's hair on fire."

"You didn't stop them?"

15

"Hell, son. I'm just one person. There are better than a dozen Hogans. Sure, I begged Rufus and Charlie to let the old Indian be, but they just laughed and warned me to mind my own business."

Zach didn't care who they were or how many relatives they had. He wouldn't back down from them or any other man. He pretended to be interested in a display of lanterns but closely watched them out of the corner of an eye, tensing when Rufus halted and stared at his bride-to-be.

Over at the dress rack, Louisa was marveling at the fashions and the colors. None were in her size, but that didn't stop her from running her fingers over the smooth material and imagining how each garment would look on her. She'd give her eyeteeth for a new dress, another reason she was tremendously intent to get to St. Louis. She would have to be properly attired when she met her aunt and the others.

"See anything you like there?"

Assuming it was the store owner who had addressed her, Lou said without looking up, "They're all so marvelous! Too bad none will fit me."

"I'm plumb surprised a squaw-girl like you has the money to afford one. What did you do, rob a white woman?"

A chill swept through Louisa. She looked up and met the gaze of a short man whose jutting chin was covered with stubble. "For your information, mister, I'm white myself."

The man snorted. "Oh, you have white skin and white hair. But those buckskins are Injun-made. And you rode in, as saucy as you please, with the buck over at the counter. That makes you an Injun lover, girl. The scum of the earth."

Lou glanced at her rifle, which she had leaned against the wall. She wasn't overly worried. A flintlock nestled snugly under her belt, so it was unlikely the two men would do more than shoot their mouths off. Then the shorter of the pair stepped up close. Lou realized he could grab her arm if she tried to draw or reach the rifle, and she began to back up. But the rack was there.

"Didn't you hear me? I said you were scum."

"I don't pay much attention to jackasses," Lou boldly informed him.

A scarlet flush crept into the short man's cheeks. "Quite a mouth you've got there. Sassy as hell. I reckon it's about time someone took you down a notch or two."

"I agree, brother," said the taller one. "Females are like dogs. When they get out of line, they have to be slapped around a bit to teach them the error of their ways." His thin mouth creased in a cruel smirk. "So which one of us is going to put this hussy in her place?"

"Neither of you." Zach had left the counter and moved soundlessly up behind them. Cold rage seethed within him, and it was all he could do to keep from shooting the two where they stood. "Stop bothering her. Now."

Rufus and Charlie Hogan turned slowly, smugly. Perhaps they were used to harmless Otoes. Perhaps they believed that no Indian would ever truly stand up to them. For neither made a move to defend himself. Sneering in contempt, they chuckled, as if the whole thing were a great joke.

"Will you look at this!" Rufus said haughtily. "The buck thinks he's the Almighty. Thinks he can tell us what we can and can't do."

"Dumb one, ain't he?" Charlie said.

"Where'd he get the gumption?" Rufus asked, feigning amazement. "He must be as drunk as a boiled owl." Making a show of sniffing, he shook his head, saying, "No, I was wrong. He hasn't touched firewater."

"He's plain dumb," Charlie reiterated.

"And too damned cocky," Rufus said. "As uppity as his white squaw." The rooster's expression crystallized into fire and hate. "Both need to learn their proper station in life. They need to be taught to show respect to their betters."

Charlie squared his shoulders. "I agree, brother. So what do we do? Whip them? Tar and feather them?"

Neither the proprietor nor the other customers had intervened, but now Slim cleared his throat and declared, "That's enough, you two. I've warned you before, Rufus, about making trouble in my place. It's bad for business."

"And we've warned you, Slim, not to meddle in our affairs. Not unless you want your precious store burned down around your ears." Rufus wagged a finger at him. "One of these days you'll really get my goat and all of us Hogans will pay you a visit."

Slim looked at Zach. "I'm sorry, but there's nothing I can do. Get your girl out of here before it's too late."

Rufus laughed. "Hell, it's *already* too late. They're not going anywhere until Charlie and I say they can." Hefting his rifle, he reached out and poked Zach in the shoulder. "And that won't be until you get down on your hands and knees."

Volcanic rage seized Zach, barely held in check through sheer force of will. "Why would I want to do that?" he asked, his features composed, giving no hint of the emotion roiling within him.

"So you can lick my boots clean. Why else?"

The brothers cackled, and it was then, when both of them were momentarily distracted, that Zach swept the Hawken's stock up and in, catching Charlie flush on the chin and felling him like a poled ox. Rufus instantly brought his own rifle into play, but he was a trifle too slow. Zach rammed the Hawken's barrel into Rufus's stomach, doubling Rufus over, then arced the stock in a half-circle that brought it crashing down on the rear of Rufus's skull. The thud of wood connecting with flesh and bone was almost as loud as the thud of Rufus's crumpled form hitting the floorboards.

Zach raised the Hawken to strike Rufus again. His next

blow would cave in the white man's head like a rotten melon. But slender fingers enclosed his wrist, and Lou sprouted in front of him.

"No! That's enough, Stalking Coyote! Don't kill him, please!"

Quivering with suppressed fury, Zach lowered the Hawken. He would much rather slay both. As any warrior could tell her, to leave an enemy alive was a mistake. Apparently, he wasn't the only one who thought so.

Slim was coming around the counter. "Were I you, ma'am, I'd let him do as he wants. Those two aren't the type to forgive and forget. Mark my words. Once they wake up, they won't rest until they've made worm food of you."

Lou dismissed the suggestion with a wave of her hand. "We'll be in St. Louis tomorrow. They'll never find us there." Not with so many people thronging the city's streets, they wouldn't. The last Lou had heard, the population had risen to a staggering sixteen thousand or better.

"I wouldn't be so sure," Slim said. "All the Hogans are part bloodhound. They can track down anyone, anywhere."

"All we need is a head start," Lou said confidently. Taking her husband-to-be's callused hand, she hurried toward the door. "Thanks for your concern, mister."

Against his better judgment, Zach let her lead him out to the hitch rail. Several riders were visible to the north. More Hogans? he wondered as he forked leather. Side by side they trotted southward, holding to a brisk pace the rest of the day. Sunset found them camped in thick undergrowth where their small fire wasn't apt to be spotted from the road.

Louisa was in merry spirits. Humming softly, she prepared stew, courtesy of a rabbit Zach had brought low with his bow and arrow, which he usually kept bundled in a blanket strapped on his mount. At the moment he was fingering a pistol and peering off through the brush at the road. Louisa grinned. "Will you quit fretting? We haven't seen any sign of them. I seriously doubt they'll chase us all over creation, no matter what Slim said. We're perfectly safe, sweetheart."

Zach made no comment. If there was one lesson his father had impressed on him more than any other, it was to never take anything for granted. Maybe the Hogans would let them be. Maybe not.

Time would tell.

Chapter Two

The Gateway to the West. Or so the city fathers of St. Louis, Missouri, boasted, and the city lived up to its reputation.

Ideally located on the west bank of the Mississippi River, St. Louis was a thriving center for pilgrims swarming to the frontier and merchandise bound for eastern outlets. The beaver trade had brought it to prominence. Over four million dollars' worth of brown gold was funneled through St. Louis before the bottom fell out of the market. The loss barely gave the growing city pause.

Its port was the pulsing heart of the rapidly expanding steamboat trade. From its wharves steamboats ranged far and wide, penetrating deep inland up the Missouri and other tributaries and downriver to the Gulf and beyond to the open sea. Business was the city's backbone. Many a merchant had grown wealthy serving as middleman for settlers thronging west and customers along the Atlantic clamoring for frontier goods.

St. Louis was not all enterprise and greed, though. The city also prided itself on its culture. Three newspapers, two bookstores, a fine theater, and half a dozen hairdressers put St. Louis in a class all by itself. Glittering mansions overlooked the wild and woolly levee district. Fancy carriages clattered along wide avenues flanked by stately trees, bearing men and women dressed in the height of fashion to plays and recitals or their favorite clubs. Rich, and proud of it, St. Louis's elite flaunted their money.

But just as there were two sides to every coin, there were also two sides to St. Louis. Her poorer districts were rife with filth and violence. In the levee district rowdy rivermen and frontiersmen caroused day and night at taverns and grogshops that catered to the rougher element. Fallen angels roved the streets in search of lustful prey. Everywhere, crime was chronic. Murder was common. Thievery rampant. Which had all led to the popular saying "God would never cross the Mississippi."

From a promontory north of the metropolis, Zachary King and Louisa May Clark gazed in astonishment at the beehive of activity. Buildings reared into the sky. The white columns of mansions gleamed among verdant trees. At berth along the wharf were scores of steamboats. Dozens more plied the river, some departing, some arriving, plumes of smoke spewing from tall, sooty smokestacks. Barges and other craft also traveled the waterway, even small canoes.

"It's fantastic!" Lou said, thinking of all the shops she could visit, the fun she would have.

Was it? Zach asked himself. He had his doubts. All those white men, every one a potential bigot. He had the feeling he was riding into a nest of rattlers. But it was too late to turn back. He was committed, come what may.

The road was heavy with traffic, wagons and riders and those on foot. Zach was pleasantly surprised to find that very few stared at him. As they neared the outskirts, he spied four Indians leaving the city on horseback. Their heads were shaved except for strips down the center, a trademark of Pawnees. In the forefront was a brawny warrior who wore a red blanket thrown over one shoulder. They showed more curiosity than hostility as they passed. None offered a word or sign in greeting.

It jogged Zach's memory. Years ago his father had clashed with the tribe over their practice of sacrificing maidens to the Morning Star. Pawnees prided themselves on being friendly to all whites, but among other tribes it was rumored they weren't above slaying a white man if they thought they could get away with it.

What were Pawness doing in St. Louis? was the big question—one Zach answered himself when he recalled that the United States government had set up something known as the Bureau of Indian Affairs there. Indians from all over were encouraged to bring their problems to the supervisor. William Clark, he of the famed Lewis and Clark expedition and an acquaintance of Zach's father, had been the first to hold the post.

"See?" Lou was saying, nodding at the backs of the Pawnees. "Indians are common here. You have nothing to worry about."

Entering the city proper was like entering a whole new world. The streets overflowed with people who always seemed to be in a hurry. Dogs, chickens, even pigs ran freely about. A riot of noise assaulted Zach's ears. Foul odors assailed his nostrils. Accustomed as he was to the order and quiet of a Shoshone village, St. Louis was sheer and utter bedlam. His dun felt the same, because it shied every so often and had to be goaded on.

Louisa beamed at everyone and everything. A flood of fond recollections washed over her. Here was the kind of life she remembered! Always on the go! Always with something to do! It thrilled her no end.

Suddenly a wagon careened around a corner. "Out of the way!" bellowed the grizzled driver, cracking a whip above his team. Pedestrians and riders alike had to scatter or be bowled over.

Zach was one of them. "Look out!" he hollered to Lou

while hauling on the reins to spur the dun to safety. Strangely enough, the wagon was empty. Zach could fathom no excuse for the driver's rude behavior. Hardly anyone else gave the rig a second glance, as if it were an everyday occurrence to almost be run over.

Lou shook her fist and was about to cast aspersions on the driver's mother when a sign ahead caught her interest. FOR LADIES ONLY, it read. Underneath was the tantalizing claim, CLOTHES FIT FOR A QUEEN. READY-MADE. Clucking to her mare, she threaded through the throng to a hitch rail.

Sighing, Zach dutifully trailed her and dismounted. Lou put her hands on his chest and kissed him lightly on the cheek.

"I won't be long. Promise."

"I'll go with you," Zach proposed.

"Silly goose. Can't you read?" Lou pointed at the sign. "It's for women only. Make yourself comfortable until I'm done." She disappeared inside.

"As you wish," Zach said. In the shade of an overhang he hunkered and draped his arms over his knees. He could squat like that for hours, as motionless as a rock, as he had demonstrated on countless hunts. To pass the time, Zach studied the passersby, a steady stream of humanity of all kinds. The well-to-do in their elaborate carriages. Beggars so poor their clothes were in tatters. Hawkish men who prowled in search of quarry. Women who wore their dresses too tight, their bodices cut too low.

There were also husbands and wives, and families with squealing kids. Lovers linked arm in arm. Youngsters in their teens, cavorting in packs. Six cavalrymen trotted by, led by a lieutenant whose uniform had been ironed to perfection and whose buttons shone like tiny suns.

To Zach it was fascinating. He would have been content to sit there for hours, but a small sign on an establishment across the street drew him to it as irresistibly as a flame drew a moth. TRAPPER'S HAVEN, it proclaimed. A tiny bell tinkled as Zach stepped into the musty interior. Traps of various manufacture hung from pegs. Rifles and pistols were on display. Virtually everything a trapper needed, fire steels and flint, axes, knives, ammunition, was on sale.

"Anyone here?" Zach ventured.

A curtain at the rear parted and out shambled an elderly man in buckskins. Hair as white as high-country snow hung in loose strands past his ears. Hobbling on a hickory walking stick, the old-timer said, "As I live and breathe, you're part Shoshone, aren't you, boy?"

Zach automatically bristled. Then he saw that the oldster was smiling and holding out a gnarled hand for him to shake. Zach did so, mentioning, "Shoshone on my mother's side. My father is Nate King."

"I'll be! I met him at the rendezvous in Willow Valley back in the early twenties. Never got to know him well, but he had a solid reputation. I'm George Milhouse." Milhouse had a firm grip for someone of his advanced years. "Have a seat, boy. Jaw a spell. It's good for these old eyes to see a young coon like yourself."

A couple of chairs were next to an unlit stove. To be sociable, Zach sank into one. He figured he had plenty of time to kill. From the way Lou talked on their journey, he got the impression she loved to shop as much as she loved being alive. She would be in the dress shop for an hour or two.

"Care for a cup of rotgut?" Milhouse asked. "I've got me a jug in the back. It'll curl your toes."

"I don't drink."

Milhouse cocked his head. "Never? That ain't hardly natural. A man has to have a few vices. They put zest in our drab lives." He eased into the other chair. "Let me guess. At your age I was mighty fond of the ladies. Couldn't keep my hands off them. They must be your particular weakness too, eh?"

"No. I'm to be married soon," Zach said.

"Oh, Lordy. Another poor soul doomed to a life of naggin'." Milhouse extended his spindly legs. "Don't get me wrong, youngster. Women are fine critters, but they do tend to weary a man. I know. I've been married four times."

"For most folks once is enough."

The old man's eyes narrowed. "You aren't one of those holier-than-thou fellers, are you? Granted, most only tie the knot once. But my first wife, a white gal, died giving birth to our baby. My second wife, a pretty Crow, was killed by the Blackfeet. My third, a Flathead, was bit by a rattler. And my fourth, a Bannock woman, died of smallpox."

Zach felt sorry for the old-timer and remarked as much, adding, "You've had some mighty bad luck in your life."

Milhouse laughed. "Hell, boy. Life is a string of bad luck broken now and again by a few spells where things go right."

"There's more to it than that."

"When I was green behind the ears I thought so, too," Milhouse said. "But the older a man gets, the more cynical he becomes. We can't help it. Life pounds us into the ground a little more each and every day, until we're buried up to our necks in grief, waitin' for that final shovelful to put us out of our misery."

Zach disagreed. "You're not taking into account all the good things life has to offer."

Placing an elbow on the chair arm and his chin in his hand, Milhouse said, "Ain't you a caution? Filled with vinegar and vim. Positive you've got all the answers. I'm the one who should feel sorry for you. Fifty years from now, sonny, you'll look back to this day and know I was right."

"Never. My pa taught me each day is a gift we're to make the most of. Fifty years from now, I hope to look back on a long, full life."

Milhouse shrugged. "Whatever pleases you. We all have our delusions." He straightened. "But enough jawin' about wishful thinkin'. Tell me the latest news from the frontier. What are the Indians up to? Any at war? And most important of all, is it true that no more rendezvous will be held?"

"It's true," Zach confirmed. The last one had been about five years before on the Green River. By then the beaver trade had dwindled to a trickle. All because silk had replaced beaver as the fashion of choice in the States. Fickle whim had done what all the hostiles and wild beasts in the wilderness couldn't.

"I'd heard as much," Milhouse said. "But I've been hopin' the market would go back to how it was. Those were grand days, boy. Livin' as we pleased. Beholden to no one. Masters of our destiny, as it were."

"You were a trapper once yourself, I take it?"

"For over ten years," Milhouse revealed. "Until those mangy Piegans caught me in their territory. I was out early one morning checkin' my line when those devils tried to sneak up on me. I dropped everything except my rifle and cut out through the woods. They gave chase, whoopin' and a-hollerin' like they do. But I was a lot more spry then than I am now. I'd have gotten clean away if not for an arrow that caught me in my left knee." Milhouse scowled. "I managed to crawl under a deadfall and hid for over eight hours while those pesky varmints searched all around me. They knew I was there somewhere. Several times they poked into the deadfall but never spotted me."

"And you say that you only have bad luck?" Zach commented.

The oldster chuckled. "Touché, as those Frenchies say. I lived, but my knee was ruined. My trappin' days were over. So I came to St. Louis and set up this shop. For a while I did brisk business. Now, with the beaver trade pretty much dead, I barely get by."

"People trap other animals."

"That's all that keeps food on my table. I've got traps for all kinds. And anything else a gent like yourself might need." Milhouse's gaze seemed to turned inward, and he said quietly, "I'll end my days here, I reckon. They'll bury me in a pauper's plot, and that will be that."

"Don't you ever look at the bright side of things?"

"I did when I was twenty. Now that I'm pushin' seventy, I can't see the sun for the clouds. So my disposition suffers." Milhouse shook himself. "But enough about me. I heard tell the Sioux tangled with the Crows last summer and killed a bunch."

There were no newspapers on the frontier. The latest information spread by word of mouth, from traveler to traveler, from campfire to campfire, or at trading posts and forts. The Sioux raid was common knowledge. Zach shared what he had heard, imparting everything of consequence about the plains and mountain tribes and certain mountain men.

"So Bridger and Walker and some of the others are guidin' settlers bound for California and the Oregon country?" Milhouse marveled. "I never thought they'd stoop so low. Oh, that I should live to see the day when seasoned coons like those two would help turn the wilds into farmland. It's downright pitiful."

"Times change. My pa says that one day there will be more homesteaders than frontiersmen."

"I hope to hell I'm dead by then. It will be the end of an era. The end of a whole way of life. The end of freedom."

"Aren't you exaggerating?" Zach asked.

"Think so? Settlers lead to towns, and towns are run by politicians, and politicians pass laws that restrict our freedom. Happens every time." Milhouse gripped his walking stick. "We've jawed so much my throat is dry. Sure I can't interest you in something to drink? Water? Coffee?"

"No, I must go." Zach had lost track of the time. "But maybe I'll come back before we leave St. Louis and let you meet my wife."

George Milhouse brightened. "Would you? That would warm my heart. I don't have any kin left, and most of my friends are nothing but bones." He shook Zach's hand again, pumping warmly. "You're welcome here anytime, son. Anytime at all."

The brightness of the afternoon forced Zach to shield his eyes from the glare with his hand. Gazing across the street, he felt his pulse quicken. The dun and the mare were gone! Alarmed, he darted into the street without thinking and was nearly trampled by a pair of riders who lashed his ears with foul language. Skirting them, he paused to let a wagon rumble by, then bounded to the empty hitch rail.

Zach's first thought was that someone must have stolen them. He scoured the street in both directions but saw no sign of either. Wondering if possibly Louisa had finished sooner than he counted on and gone in search of him, he hastened into the clothing store. Five women were browsing or gaily chatting among neatly arranged shelves and racks. Every last one immediately stopped what they were doing to stare.

"What on earth are *you* doing in here?" From around a tall rack of dresses walked a brunette in her thirties, elegantly dressed, her luxurious hair done up in a bun. She held a measuring tape and a piece of chalk.

"I'm hunting for my fiancée," Zach said. "She came in here a while ago. Her name is Lou."

"Your fiancée?" the brunette sniffed. "I don't cater to squaws. Didn't you see the sign?" She indicated a small one tacked up near the door: NO INDIANS ALLOWED.

"She's white," Zach said. "About my age. Louisa May Clark. You must remember her."

"No one by that name has been here," the woman stated coldly.

"But I saw her come in," Zach said. "You couldn't miss her. She was wearing buckskins."

"And I tell you that no one answering that description has paid me a visit." The brunette motioned. "Now, I'll thank you to leave. You're disturbing the other ladies."

Zach would do no such thing. "Lou!" he shouted. "Where are you?" Some of the women tittered. When there was no reply, Zach stepped to the head of the next aisle. "Lou! Lou!"

Shaking the chalk at him, the brunette advanced. "That will be quite enough! You're making a scene. Go now, or you'll be sorry."

"I'm not leaving until I find out where she is," Zach declared. "Maybe someone else who works here remembers her."

29

"I'm Sylvia Banner, and this is my establishment. I have no employees." Banner put her hands on her hips and said quite loudly, "Now, for the last time, I'm asking you to go. Make a spectacle of yourself somewhere else."

Zach started down the aisle. He would tear the store apart, if need be, to find a clue to Lou's whereabouts. At that juncture a door on the left opened and in strode two big men in overalls, carrying clubs.

"About time," Sylvia Banner said. "Were you two lummoxes sleeping again?"

"No, ma'am," said an ox whose right cheek bore a zigzag scar. "We came as soon as we heard you." His dull gaze shifted to Zach. "Is this vermin giving you grief? Say the word and Titus and me will bust up half the bones in his body."

Some of the other women smiled at the prospect, but Banner shook her head. "Only if the savage won't be reasonable. I don't want blood splattered all over the clothes." She wagged the tape measure. "So what will it be, young man? Will you leave quietly, or must I have you thrown out on your red ear?"

The man with the scar moved toward him but stopped dead when Zach raised the Hawken. "I just want to find my fiancée."

"Then I suggest you look elsewhere. As you can see, she isn't here." Sylvia Banner seemed to soften. "Perhaps she did come in, as you claim. But if so, she didn't stay long. And if I was busy with another customer, I might not have noticed."

Her explanation was logical enough. Zach worried that he had blundered badly, that Lou had gone back out shortly after he stepped into Milhouse's, and after waiting awhile, she had gone to look for him. She must be frantic, afraid something had happened to him. He lowered the rifle but didn't take his eyes off the pair with the clubs. "I'll go. I'm sorry for disturbing you."

"No real harm done," Banner said. "And if your fiancée

30

does show up, I'll make it a point to mention you stopped by." She paused. "Where will you be? At the Indian agency? Or are you staying with friends?"

"We just arrived," Zach said. "We don't have a place to stay yet." Backing out, he moved to the end of the boardwalk and pondered what to do. St. Louis was immense, covering many square miles. One person couldn't possibly cover the entire city in less than a month. How was he to find her?

Zach needed advice. And the only individual he knew capable of giving it to him was the old trapper. Winding through the traffic, he barreled into the Trapper's Haven and discovered Milhouse still in the chair by the stove, sipping on a silver flask.

"Well, well. Ain't this a surprise. Miss my company already? Or did you think of something you need to buy?"

"I've lost my fiancée," Zach said, and quickly related what had occurred. "I need to know how best to locate her." A story his father liked to tell about an incident in New York City gave him an idea, and he asked, "Do they have constables here? My pa told me they help people in situations like this."

Milhouse rose, capped the flask, and slid it into a pocket. "The mayor and the aldermen got around to organizin' a police force back in '39, as I recollect. It's not much to speak of, though. Most of the constables are too lazy to give a damn. The rest are paid under the table to look the other way when crimes are committed."

"So you're saying it wouldn't do any good?"

"Oh, if you had a hundred dollars or so you might get one or two to poke around and ask a few questions."

"I only have ten," Zach said. Lou was carrying most of their money, forty dollars they had been given by his parents as a gift. "But I'll spend every penny if it will help."

"It could." The old trapper walked to the small window. His brow knitting, he scratched his chin and kept saying softly to himself, "I wonder. I wonder."

"You wonder what?" Zach was impatient to do something. To do *anything*. He was plagued by the thought he might not be able to find Lou, that their separation might be permanent. Every minute they wasted was crucial.

A shaft of sunlight bathed George Milhouse, lending his pale features an even more ghostly aspect. "I'm wonderin' about another young feller who rushed in here about seven or eight months ago. He'd lost his filly, too. Said she went into the dress shop and never came out. He contacted the constables, but they couldn't find hide nor hair of that girl."

"Did they tear the city up looking for her?"

"Not quite. Hell, son, folks disappear all the time. Runaways. Discontented wives and husbands. But for two young women to go missin' in the same store is a mite odd, even by St. Louis standards." Milhouse smacked his palm against his thigh. "And now that I think about it, there is that black van that rolls up behind the dress shop late at night on occasion. It must all be connected. I should have seen the truth sooner."

Zach wished the man would talk sense. "What truth?"

"I'd rather not say until I'm certain. The best thing for us to do is wait—"

Zach had heard enough. "You expect me to sit here and do nothing?" He barged toward the door, half convinced the old man was babbling nonsense. He would head up the street, deeper into the city, and ask along the way if anyone had seen a woman answering to Lou's description. Not that many white women favored buckskins. Someone was bound to have noticed her.

"Hold on, now." For someone his age, Milhouse could move swiftly when he wanted. He barred the way, thrusting his free hand out. "I need for you to trust me. I know I'm askin' a lot, since we've just met. But if I'm right, you'll have your fiancée back before the sun rises tomorrow."

"I can't wait that long." Zach gripped the old man's shoulder to push him aside.

"Please listen," Milhouse pleaded. "For her sake if not

for your own." He became gravely somber. "You don't know this city like I do. It's filled with wickedness. Sodom and Gomorrah rolled into one. Every kind of sin you can imagine, and some you can't."

"What does that have to do with Louisa?"

"Everything. The papers are full of stories about young gals forced into a life of ill repute." Milhouse looked into Zach's eyes. "You do know what a prostitute is, don't you? A woman who sells her body for money?"

"A—?" Zach couldn't bring himself to say it. "But Lou has never—" They had wanted to, dearly, but they had agreed to wait until they were wed.

Milhouse nodded. "Exactly the sort that fetches the highest price. It saddens me terribly to suggest this, son. I can see how hurt you are. But there's a very good chance your filly has fallen into the clutches of the worst criminal element in all of St. Louis."

Zach broke out in a cold sweat. "Say it straight, old-timer."

"I fear your precious Lou has been kidnapped."

Chapter Three

Louisa May Clark took two bouncy steps into the dress shop, then drew up short. The selection was astounding. Dresses were lined up in long rows, dresses hung on racks against all four walls, dresses had been pinned to the ceiling for display. She had died and gone to dress heaven!

Only two other customers were in the store. As Lou came to the rack she sought, a door on the left wall opened and in sashayed a brunette attired in a crisp new dress, her hair in a bun. The newcomer saw Lou and reacted as if someone had pricked her with a pin. Smiling broadly, the woman came over.

"Well, well. What have we here? I'm Sylvia Banner, the owner. Who might you be, young lady?"

Louisa liked being called a lady. She gave her name and said, "I'm in powerful need of a new dress. Something nice. I want to impress my in-laws."

"Is that so?" Banner looked Lou up and down. "If you don't mind my saying, you must be fresh off the prairie. I don't see many ladies wearing buckskin these days, not unless they're Indians, of course."

"I've come from the Rockies," Lou said, flipping through some dresses. "I'm here with my fiancé to meet relatives from Ohio."

Banner scanned the shop. "I don't see him."

"Oh, he's waiting outside. Your sign said women only." Lou found a dress she liked and took it from the rack to examine it.

"Men gripe too much," Banner said. "They complain when their wife or companion is taking too long, or buying a garment that costs too much. But I guess I don't need to tell you how *men* are."

They both laughed, and soon Banner was sharing the story of her life, how she had opened the shop four years before after serving as an apprentice dressmaker. And how her business was slowly but steadily improving as word of mouth of her wide selection and fair prices spread. "But I don't mind admitting, Louisa, it's a struggle to make ends meet. Sometimes I have to supplement my income in ways I'd rather not."

Lou had decided the first dress wasn't suitable and was holding another up in front of a mirror. "How do you mean?"

"Oh, a little of this, a little of that," Banner said, and laughed. "But enough about me. I want to hear all about you."

"There's not much to tell."

"Oh, come now. You've lived in the mountains. You must have seen many interesting sights, done many interesting things." Banner paused. "You say your fiancé is outside? Is he a big, strapping frontiersman?"

"He's the son of a mountain man."

"You don't say? And the two of you crossed the plains all alone?"

"That we did," Lou said proudly. "It was rough, but Zach—that's his name—he's the best hunter and tracker who ever lived. His pa gave him a map showing where all the rivers and streams are, so we never had to go more than a couple of days without water."

"He sounds like quite a fellow. I'd like to meet him."

"Would you really?" Lou said, pleased by Banner's friendliness. "Wait right here." Scooting to the front door, she opened it. To her dismay, Zach wasn't there. She checked the street in vain. Disappointed, Lou rejoined Banner. "He must have wandered off, darn him."

"That's a man for you. They hate to shop. Don't be too upset. He'll return sooner or later."

"He shouldn't have done it." Lou had flattered herself that Zach was so devoted, he would wait forever. It hurt a smidgen to learn he was just like every other man.

Banner fiddled with buttons on a calico dress. "What about those relatives you mentioned? How come none of them are helping you?"

"Oh, they don't even know we've arrived yet," Lou said. "I aim to surprise them tonight wearing a brand-new dress."

"I'll help you pick one that's just right," Banner offered.

"You're awful kind," Lou responded, "but what about your other customers?"

"If they need help, they'll yell."

For the next half an hour Lou inspected dress after dress. Several struck her fancy, but Sylvia Banner pointed out flaws in each. One didn't complement her hair. Another was too loose at the waist. The third made her shoulders look too boyish. Lou began to despair of ever finding one that would be suitable.

Banner chatted about St. Louis, about the deplorable condition of the streets. How a lady couldn't walk two blocks without dirtying her shoes. When it rained, many of the thoroughfares turned to mud. The only safe means to get around was by carriage.

Lou kept hoping Zach would peer in the window or enter to check on her. Vaguely, she was aware when other women came and went. Usually there was at least one other customer. She didn't think much about it until Banner's hand fell on her shoulder.

"We're alone at last."

Lou gazed around. Sure enough, they were. "I guess I should be on my way too," she remarked. There were bound to be more shops, and one was bound to have the perfect dress for her.

Banner glanced at the window, then at the door in the left wall. "You know, I've been thinking. I've been terribly remiss. Just yesterday I received a shipment of new dresses from Philadelphia. The latest fashions."

"Why don't you have them on display?" Lou asked.

"I haven't had the time." Banner smiled sweetly. "Usually I don't let my customers in the storage room. But you're a special case. So how about if I allow you to go through the new assortment before anyone else? You can take your pick. And if your fiancé shows up, I'll bring him to you."

"You'd do that for me?"

"Why not? Anything for a customer, I always say." Banner moved to the door, opened it just wide enough to stick her head in, and bobbed her head. Then she turned and glanced at the entrance again. "All right. Have fun. The dresses are straight ahead. I've got to stay out here in case someone comes in."

Banner stepped aside. Lou started to push the door all the way open, then remembered something. "Oh. I left my rifle over by the rack. I'd better fetch it."

"No, you go on in," Banner insisted. "I'll get it for you. That fiancé of yours could show up any second, and you don't want to keep him waiting."

"Thanks again." Lou couldn't wait to inform Zach how nice Banner was. Not all whites were spiteful. She entered the storage room and went a couple of feet, stopping in consternation when she didn't see any dresses or packing crates or anything. The room contained a table and two chairs and a cot with a rope coiled under it against the far wall. On the table were a coffeepot and two cups, as well as a deck of cards. Some of the cards were spread out, facedown, as if someone had been playing a game and been interrupted. "What in the world?" She heard the door shut.

As Lou began to swivel, steely arms encircled her from behind, pinning her own. For an instant she was too startled too do anything. Then another man, a brute with a scar on his cheek, came from behind and lifted a strip of cloth toward her mouth to gag her. Galvanized by fear, Lou kicked him, catching him in the groin. The brute grunted and staggered backward. She opened her mouth to scream, but the man holding her pressed a hand over her mouth.

"Please don't make a sound!"

Lou bit him, shearing her teeth through skin and flesh. He stifled a yelp, then hurled her bodily to the floor. Lou landed on her side, the breath whooshing from her lungs. She clawed at her pistol, but the man she had bit was on her before she could draw, his knee gouging into her ribs as he sought to pin her and wrest the flintlock from her grasp. Lou struggled for all she was worth, tugging and punching and thrashing.

"I need help here, Erskine!" the man called out. "This girl is a regular wildcat."

The scarred brute was lumbering toward them. "Hold your britches on, Titus." He balled his enormous fists, the knuckles like knots on a tree. "One tap is all it will take."

Lou was losing her battle for control of the pistol. "Sylvia!" she screeched. "I'm being attacked! Get help!" Lou figured that the men had broken into the store, intending to either rob or violate Banner.

Erskine reared over her. "Feisty but stupid." He cocked an arm. "Aren't you in for a surprise when you wake up!"

A knotty fist streaked toward Lou's chin. Titus had hold of the flintlock and her other wrist and was straddling her, but she could still move, could still twist her head at the very last second. Erskine's big fist slammed into the floor-boards, eliciting a howl.

"Hold her still, damn it!"

"I'm trying," Titus said. "She's slippery as an eel!"

Lou suddenly swept her legs up, locking her feet against Titus's neck. She rocked to one side, then the other, gaining momentum. Titus sputtered and shook his head like a mastiff trying to shake off a terrier, but she refused to be denied. As Erskine raised his other fist, Lou pumped the lower half of her body, leverage succeeding where strength would not. She flipped Titus clean off.

Erskine drove his fist at Lou's chest, but she rolled to the left and heaved to her feet. She had lost her grip on the pistol, but she still had a Green River knife at her waist and she resorted to it now, the blade flashing out just as Erskine tried to close with her. He leaped back, narrowly evading the razor edge.

Titus was rising and rubbing his neck. "Give up, girl, and we won't hurt you."

"Like hell we won't!" Erskine rasped. "I owe her for that kick!"

The door burst inward. In rushed Sylvia Banner in a state of agitation. "What is all the ruckus?"

"Run, Sylvia!" Louisa cried. "You're in danger!"

But the woman didn't heed. Instead, she slammed the door and glowered at the two men. "What the hell is going on? I had to put the CLOSED sign on the front door, you're making so much racket!"

"Don't blame us," Titus said. "She's a hellion. We're trying our best."

"Try harder!" Banner rotated toward Lou. "Make this easy on yourself. Do as we want and no harm will come to you. I give you my word. Festerman doesn't pay for damaged merchandise."

Lou was bewildered by the stunning turn of events. "You're in cahoots with them? But what's this all about? Why are you doing this to me?"

"It has nothing to do with you personally," Banner said. "Think of it as a business transaction. Festerman is always in the market for new flesh to peddle." She sighed. "I told you it's hard for me to make ends meet. So I earn extra income by selling an occasional girl to him."

"Sell?" Lou repeated, the full horror of her plight commencing to dawn. "And you've done this to others?" Outrage filled her, and a sense of terrible betrayal. Elevating the knife, she sprang at Banner, fully intending to bury it in the woman's heart. But she reckoned without Titus and Erskine, who had been waiting for just such an opportunity. They converged. She struck at Erskine, but the scarred man blocked her forearm and rammed his fist into the pit of her stomach.

Pinpoints of brilliant light exploded in front of Lou's eyes. The room spun, the figures in it lost in a dazzling haze. She was roughly seized, the knife ripped free. Someone carried her, then unceremoniously dumped her onto her back. Her wrists were gripped and rope wound tight. She tried to resist, but she was too woozy, too weak.

"Go easy on her, Erskine," Sylvia Banner said. "I don't want her bruised any more than she already is."

"If it were up to me, I'd knock her senseless," the scarred man replied.

"It's not up to you. Any more sass and I'll find someone to replace you." Banner's shoes clacked on the floor, and the door squeaked. "I've got to open up again before her fiancé shows up. Gag her. Make sure she doesn't make a sound."

"Don't worry," Erskine said.

Lou's vision began to clear. She saw both men above her and realized she was on the cot. Titus started to bind her ankles.

Erskine scowled. "Since the boss lady doesn't want bruises, there won't be bruises. But I'll be damned if I'm letting you get away with what you did." So saying, he smashed his fist into her stomach again.

This time Lou was swept into an inky vortex. Her consciousness faded, and the last thing she heard was Erskine.

"That serves the bitch right."

A cool sensation on Louisa's brow revived her. She opened her eyes with a start and tried to sit up, but she had been tied to the cot. Loops of rope were across her chest and legs.

"We're not taking any chances with you, not after the aggravation you caused my boys," Sylvia Banner said. Banner had pulled a chair next to the cot and was dabbing a folded cloth in a glass of water. "I'll remove the gag for a while if you give me your word you won't scream."

Lou would have given anything for the chance to slam the woman's head into a wall.

"It won't do you any good if you do. You've been out for hours. The shop is closed, and these walls are thick. No one is likely to hear you." Banner pressed the cloth to Lou's forehead. "Will you behave?"

As long as it suited Lou, she would. She nodded, and the brunette promptly undid the knots. Lou moved her mouth to restore some of the feeling. Erskine had tied the gag so tight, her lips were partly numb.

"As for your fiancée," Banner said, "you can forget about him rescuing you. He finally did come by a while after we snared you. I assured him I had never seen you."

"Zach would never believe that!" Lou declared.

"On the contrary, little one. I'd imagine he's combing the city right this moment, out of his mind with worry. Tomorrow he'll think to check here again, but by then you'll be long gone." Banner placed the glass down. "I, of course, will sympathize with his plight and volunteer to do whatever I can to help find you."

"You're evil through and through."

Banner chortled. "How naive you are, child. Evil has nothing to do with it. Necessity is the ruler of our fates. In my case, the necessity to pay off creditors and to live in the style to which I have grown accustomed."

41

David Thompson

Lou tried to rise onto her elbows but couldn't. "How many women have you done this to?"

"I've never counted them," Banner said. "But I'd guess an average of one every two months for the past three years." She sat up. "It's easy money. St. Louis is rife with lost waifs and bumpkins like you just in from the frontier. Festerman pays top dollar for your kind."

Titus and Erskine were playing cards. Lou saw her weapons piled on the table to one side, and longed to get her hands on her knife. "Who's this Festerman character you keep talking about?"

"Lon Festerman. One of the richest men in the city. He owns a bunch of bawdy houses frequented by the well-to-do." Banner stretched, arching her spine like a cat. "His clients are willing to pay through the nose for the privilege of making love to innocents like you. Which is why Festerman will pay me five hundred dollars when I turn you over to him."

"You'll get caught one day," Lou predicted. "The law will round all of you up, toss you into prison, and throw away the key."

"Oh, please. Festerman has half the constables in the city in his back pocket." Banner brushed at a stray wisp of hair that had escaped her bun. "You have a lot to learn about life, my young friend."

"I'm not your friend, and I never will be."

"Don't be so sure. Once you find out how much money you can make, you might thank me for this."

Lou couldn't believe what she was hearing. "You're demented. I'd kill myself before I'd allow any man to paw me. Festerman can't make me do something against my will."

Banner and her cohorts broke into hearty mirth. "I'm afraid you're wrong there, too. A few doses of opium and you'll be eating out of Lon's hand. You'll do anything he asks, just to have more. Even sleep with perfect strangers."

"Never!" Lou quivered with pent-up resentment. "Is that

42

what he did to all the others? Drugged them? And you stood by and did nothing?"

"How many times must I tell you? I'm in this for the money." Banner slowly stood. "Besides, even if I wanted to, there's little I could do. Festerman has over fifty cut-throats at his beck and call."

"You're real good at making excuses for yourself, aren't you, lady?"

Flushing, Banner backhanded Lou across the face, then raised her hand to do it again. But she didn't. "Damn you, girl. You're so high and mighty. Think you know it all. But life isn't as clear-cut as you make it out to be. Sometimes we do things we might not like doing but we have to. We're not left any choice."

Lou grew hot with indignation. "We always have a choice. I'll die before I let a man violate me."

"A fate worse than death, eh?" Banner mocked her. "Well, we'll see. But I'm willing to wager that a year from now you won't recognize yourself. You'll be prancing around in silk dresses, catering to the whims of randy rich men. See if you don't." Turning on a heel, Banner walked off. She tossed the gag onto the table, saying, "If the girl behaves, let her be. If she makes so much as a peep, stuff this down her throat."

"With pleasure," Erskine said.

Tears welled up in Lou's eyes, but she fought them, resisting a tide of despair and anxiety. Nate King always liked to say, "Where there's a will, there's a way." There *had* to be a way out of the fix she was in. As long as she kept her wits about her, she would find it.

And there was Zach. Lou knew him. Believed in him. Trusted him. He loved her with the breadth and depth of his soul. He wouldn't rest until he had turned St. Louis upside down seeking her. Banner might have thrown him off the scent, but he would be back.

Thinking of Zach calmed Lou considerably. He always incited such wonderful feelings. Love, awe, thankfulness.

When she was with him, she felt as if she were complete. A strange way to describe it, yet appropriate. He filled an emptiness in her, a great longing she hadn't realized was there until he came into her life. Maybe it was the same with everyone who fell in love. She couldn't say. She only knew that she cared for him as much as he cared for her, and nothing could ever keep them apart for long. They wouldn't let it.

A shadow fell across her. Titus appeared, nervously fidgeting. "Would you like some coffee? Or a bite to eat?"

Over at the table, Erskine swore. "She doesn't deserve a crumb or a single drop. Not after what the witch did to me. Leave her be."

Titus stayed put. "The girl was doing what anyone would. Trying to save herself. You can't blame her for that." Bending, he asked, "So what would you like? You must be awful thirsty and hungry. Miss Banner won't mind."

Lou hadn't given any thought to nourishment, but her throat did feel parched. "Coffee, I suppose. Unless you can get some water."

Nodding, Titus tramped to the table and filled his own cup.

Erskine, irritated, was shuffling the cards, smacking them down between riffles. "You softhearted simpleton. Why bother? In another five or six hours the van will be here. Let Festerman's boys take care of her."

Lou's interest was piqued. "What van?"

"Every time we snare a new prize, Banner sends word to Festerman and he sends a van to pick them up. Late at night, so no one is likely to notice." Erskine began to deal. "Lon is one sly fox. He doesn't miss a trick."

Titus brought the cup and sat in the chair. "I'll have to help you," he said. "Miss Banner would beat me with a broom if I untied you."

"I'm obliged for your kindness," Lou said.

Titus actually blushed and averted his eyes. "Shucks. I'd do the same for any lady. I'm real sorry about what we've done to you, but it's how I earn my living. I have a wife and five sprouts to feed."

Erskine snickered. "Tell her your life's story, why don't you? I swear. A turnip has more brains than you do. I could knock you for a row of houses, you get me so mad."

Leaning lower, Titus whispered to Louisa, "Pay him no mind. He's always as prickly as a scalded cat." Titus raised the cup to her mouth, carefully tilting it so coffee trickled between her lips. "You're one of the youngest we've caught so far. As I recall, the only girl younger was a fourteen-year-old."

Lou swallowed, then said, "How can you do this to people? A married man like you? You don't seem half bad otherwise."

"Thank you, ma'am." Titus swelled at the praise. "I try to be nice about it. My grandma always said that if a man can't do anything else with his life, he should always be nice to folks. She ought to know. She was the sweetest lady who ever lived."

"Doesn't your conscience ever bother you?" Lou bluntly asked.

"I can't say as it does, to be honest. It's not as if I'm hurting anyone. Mr. Festerman sets his women up in fancy rooms, with a lot of new clothes and all that other stuff womenfolk admire. They go for carriage rides every day and attend balls and such every night. It's a fine life, if you ask me. Finer than mine."

Erskine growled like a vicious mongrel. "You should be a Bible-thumper, Titus. Then you could help people all you want."

"I can't read," Titus said. "I couldn't quote scripture like preachers do."

A fit of laughter hit Erskine. When it subsided, he looked at Lou. "Ask him for a steak supper with all the trimmings. Or a couple of pillows and a quilt. Knowing him, he'd get them."

Titus lowered the cup to Lou again. "You shouldn't pick on me like that, pard. I treat you nice, too, don't I? Haven't I taken you to my home for meals? Didn't I give you that shirt for your birthday?"

"Shut up," Erskine snapped.

Lou sipped slowly, racking her mind for a means to escape. She considered playing on Titus's sympathies, but so long as Erskine was there, it wouldn't work. Without being obvious, she wriggled her wrists and twisted her ankles, testing how much play there was in the ropes. There wasn't any. She might be able to free herself if she had half a day in which to do it, and if no one was guarding her.

Hour after hour dragged by. Her captors played poker, using wood slivers to bet with. Erskine's surly disposition became worse when he fell into a losing streak. Eventually he threw his cards down in disgust and began to pace like a caged mountain lion.

"It was only a game," Titus ventured. "I won't hold you to the money you owe me, if that's what has you out of sorts."

"I wasn't going to pay anyway." Erskine walked to the cot and leered at Louisa. "I could sure use some female cuddling right about now, to relax me. What do you say, smooth cheeks?"

"Stop that," Titus said.

Erskine whirled on his friend as if to assault him, then froze when the door opened and in strolled Sylvia Banner. "The time has come. The van is here."

Chapter Four

Waiting was not one of Zachary King's favorite pastimes. Oh, when he was after game he could hunker as motionless as a boulder for hours on end near a game trail or spring. But when he was anxious to do something, he couldn't bear to sit around waiting to get it done. In this particular instance his impatience was made worse by the peril his beloved was in. He couldn't bear to sit in the dark in George Milhouse's store, waiting.

The old trapper was taking his turn at the window. "This reminds me of the time the Bloods stole a cache of my plews. Or half of it, anyhow. My partner and me expected them to return for the rest, so we hid ourselves in some brush. We couldn't so much as sneeze for fear they'd be sneakin' up on us and hear."

Zach grunted. The oldster had been rambling on since sunset, and it was now past midnight. He would much rather wait in silence. But Milhouse liked to chatter as much as a chipmunk. It would take a fist to the teeth to shut him up.

David Thompson

"So there we were, son, in the dead of night, lyin' as still as you please, when I felt a snake crawl onto my leg. I figured it was a rattler, since they do most of their huntin' after dark. But I didn't dare look, didn't dare move, not when it might strike. All I could do was lay there like a log hopin' it would slither off. Thing was, though, it liked the warmth my body gave off, so it crawled higher and made itself to home."

Despite himself, Zach inquired, "What did you do?"

"What else could I do? I waited until it crawled up on my backside, then I farted and blew it to pieces." Laughter spilled from Milhouse, laughter that was contagious.

Sharing tall tales qualified as a mountaineer tradition. Zach's father claimed it got its start at the early rendezvous, when trappers gathered to compare experiences. A little exaggeration for humor's sake was expected. Some of the mountain men were so adept at storytelling, sometimes it was impossible to tell where the lie ended and the truth began.

Zach remembered listening to an exchange between Jim Bridger—or Old Gabe, as the trappers called him—and Joe Meek. When Meek bragged about a "rainbow bird" he had supposedly seen, so named because every feather was a different color of the rainbow, Bridger told a whopper of his own to outdo Meek. It seems that once on a trek west, Bridger had stumbled on a forest of petrified trees in which petrified birds warbled petrified songs.

"Once, up in Snake country," Milhouse continued, "I was coming around a narrow trail when I ran into a griz. A huge she-bear. Well, I didn't hardly want to shoot. It would only make her mad, and I had nowhere to run. So I opened a parfleche and took out a swatch of red cloth I'd bought for a Flathead lovely I was fond of. I held it out for the she-bear to sniff and admire."

"Did she attack you?"

"On the contrary, son. The next time I saw her, that she-bear was usin' it as a shawl and struttin' around as pretty as you please."

48

"I haven't heard that one before," Zach said, grinning. "You should write them down for posterity."

"Who'd want to read them? No one gives a hoot about the old days."

Zach did. He liked to hear about the adventures his father and mother had. His pa was keeping a journal, and maybe one day it would be made into a book, as the exploits of some of the other mountaineers had been.

One of Zach's secret passions was reading. Ever since he was knee-high to a cricket, his father had read to him every evening. Three whole shelves in their cabin were devoted to nothing but books. The latest from James Fenimore Cooper. *Ivanhoe,* by Scott. And many more.

"That's one of the great tragedies of life, boy. Old people are filled with wisdom and experience, but young people don't want to hear any of it. They have to go through the same experiences and learn the same wisdom before they're willing to listen. And by then, they're old themselves, and cycle starts all over again."

"Anyone ever mention how you talk in circles?" Zach teased.

"All my wives," Milhouse said. "Except for the Bannock. We communicated mostly in sign."

"You didn't bother to learn her tongue?"

"She was deaf."

Zach jabbed a finger at the window. "Any sign of that van yet? You said it would be here by now."

"Don't get your dander up. Some nights it arrives later than others. If it weren't for the fact I don't hardly need but three hours' sleep a night anymore, I'd never have spotted it. Until today I figured it was making deliveries, that whoever owned it wanted to avoid all the traffic during the day. Now I suspect that's not the case."

"When it comes, you let me take care of things."

Milhouse looked at him. "Not on your life, sonny. This is the first excitement I've had since I left the Rockies. It's my notion, so I want in."

49

"She's my fiancée," Zach said.

"And I won't do anything to put her in more danger than she already is," the trapper promised. "I won't make a move unless you say so."

"I don't know . . ."

"Think for a moment. You'll need someone to watch your back, and I'm the only candidate. Unless you'd rather rely on a constable. I should warn you, though, that they have a habit of being the first to flatten when guns go off."

Zach was still against the idea. Milhouse was well past his prime. The man couldn't take three steps without his walking stick. If they got into trouble, Milhouse couldn't run. "I don't want your blood on my hands."

"It's my blood. I can bleed as I see fit." Milhouse was annoyed. "My mettle hasn't been tested in a coon's age. I won't let you or anyone else deny me a little fun."

"Even if the fun, as you call it, gets you killed?"

The trapper had more to say, but the clatter of hooves and the creaking of a wagon nipped his argument in the bud. He peeked out the window, then beckoned. "At last! Just like I said."

Keeping low, Zach dashed to the wall and raised his eyes to the sill. A long black van was nearing the dress shop. The driver and another were perched on the seat. Yellow letters were painted on the side, but it was too dark for Zach to read them. He watched as the driver skillfully wheeled the van into a narrow alley between the dress shop and the next building. The van disappeared behind the shop.

"Off we go," Milhouse said excitedly, hobbling toward the door.

"Off I go," Zach corrected him, darting past the old trapper and running into the night. In a burst of speed he reached the opposite side of the street, and the shop. At the corner he stopped to listen. Muffled voices gave no clue to what was taking place. On silent soles he glided to the rear, slowing as he came to the next corner. A door slammed, smothering the voices.

Zach looked before committing himself. A rutted dirt

yard flanked the shop. The van had been parked so the back end was several feet from a door. A lantern on a peg illuminated the lettering on the side. LON'S SWEETMEATS, Zach read. SWEETEST IN ST. LOUIS. It made no sense to him. He was about to step into the open when the door opened and out strode the driver and his partner. Trailing them was Sylvia Banner.

". . . get full credit for this one. She's as green as grass, Horace. Just the kind Lon is always looking for."

"Have I ever shorted you?" the driver responded. "I've marked it in the tally book, which no one but Mr. Festerman ever touches. He'll send the money by messenger, the day after tomorrow at the latest."

The driver's partner pulled a large key from his pocket and inserted it into a lock on the back of the van. A narrow door opened. From it wafted soft sobbing and a woman's groans.

"How many do you have in there tonight?" Sylvia Banner asked.

"Yours will make the fifth," Horace said. "Two local runaways, a gal from New York City who came to St. Louis all by her lonesome on a steamboat, and a pilgrim bound for California who strayed from the rest of her party." Horace patted the van's door. "Not a bad haul, if I do say so myself. Usually we're lucky to get this many in a month."

The driver's partner moved toward the front. "We should hurry up, Horace. We're running late as it is."

Banner turned and snapped her fingers. "Erskine! Titus! What's keeping you? Get her out here."

Zach's breath caught in his throat when the two big men who had menaced him in the shop appeared. Not because of them, but because of the bound figure in their grip. Louisa was slumped over, her feet dragging. A gag covered her mouth, and she was panting as if she'd just sprinted a mile.

"Don't blame us," Erskine said. "This damn hellcat started kicking the second we cut her loose of the cot."

"He punched her," Titus said.

51

The brunette clucked like an ill-tempered hen. "I thought I made it clear. No bruises! Not a one."

"Don't lay an egg. I only hit her hard enough to quiet her down," Erskine said.

A red haze seemed to envelop the yard and the people in it. Zach felt his temples pound to the beat of his own blood and heard a great rush of sound in his ears, like the driving rhythm of rapids. His moccasins moved of their own accord. Pointing the Hawken at Erskine and Titus, he growled, "That's far enough!"

Everyone imitated tree stumps except the driver's partner. His right hand dove under his coat and snaked out, holding a derringer. As he brought it up to shoot, a glimmer of silver sliced the air. None of them was more surprised than Zach when a knife embedded itself in the partner's wrist. Blood spurted in a geyser. Crying out, the man dropped the derringer and clasped the wrist to his chest.

"That'll teach him," George Milhouse said, materializing as if out of nowhere. In his left hand was a .55-caliber smoothbore pistol. "Now, which one of these scoundrels wants to be next?"

"You!" Banner exclaimed. "What on earth are you doing, Milhouse?"

Horace, the driver, was coiled to spring. "You know him? Who the hell is he, your grandpa?"

"He owns a store across from mine," Banner said. "I've talked to him once or twice. Always took him to be a harmless old coot."

Milhouse chuckled. "Figured wrong, didn't you, hussy?" He trained the flintlock on the driver. "I once slew a Piegan war chief with this. It blew a hole in him the size of an apple. Care for a demonstration?"

Zach was mad at the trapper for not listening. But he had a more urgent concern—namely, Louisa. Erskine and Titus were still holding her. "Untie her, damn you!" He moved forward, the pounding in his head growing louder with each step. When neither moved, he leaped and smashed the stock against the one with the scar. Erskine crumpled, a scarlet rivulet seeping from a nasty gash. "I won't say it again!" He was ready to slay them all if they didn't obey.

Titus glanced at Sylvia Banner. "Do as he says," she instructed, and Titus sank onto a knee.

Banner rounded on Zach. "You've just made the worst mistake of your life, savage. No one bucks Lon Festerman. He'll have you hunted down and stomped into a greasy smear."

"He'll have to wait in line," Zach said, remembering the Hogans. Titus was prying at the knots, but not doing it fast enough to suit him. Impatient, Zach nudged Titus with the Hawken's muzzle. "Hurry up!"

"Son! The other one—!"

Milhouse's warning came a fraction of a second too late. Erskine had surged up off the ground, producing a knife from under his shirt—Louisa's Green River knife, which Erskine thrust at Zach's ribs. By the width of a whisker, Zach evaded it by wrenching aside. He whipped the barrel against Erskine's temple, but it didn't have any effect.

Growling like a feral beast, Erskine pounced, grabbing for the rifle with one hand while lancing the knife at Zach. To save himself, Zach seized the man's wrist. Then they were down, grappling, rolling back and forth. Erskine's grip on the Hawken prevented Zach from swinging it, while Zach's hold on Erskine's wrist kept the blade at bay. But it wouldn't for long. Erskine was a full-grown man, Zach a stripling. Erskine outweighed Zach by sixty or seventy pounds. Gradually, the knife inched toward its target.

Zach flipped to the right, to the left. His foe continued to push the knife nearer, ever nearer. He arced his knee up, but it struck Erskine's leg instead of where it would hurt the most. Erskine returned the favor, but Zach anticipated as much and shifted just enough to deflect the brunt of the blow.

Zach glimpsed Milhouse, covering the others. Given the situation, it was all the trapper could do. To try and shoot Erskine was too risky, what with the constant shifting and rolling. The slug might core the wrong one. So Zach was on his own. He had to end it, and end it quickly.

To do so, Zach resorted to a tactic he'd seen a Shoshone warrior by the name of Touch the Clouds use. Zach drove his forehead into Erskine's face, into the man's nose. Cartilage crunched, and wet drops spattered Zach's cheeks.

A howl of rage and pain was torn from Erskine, but he didn't let go of the knife as Zach had hoped. No, the scarred brute redoubled his effort to sink it in Zach, throwing all of his superior weight into the attempt.

The tip of the blade touched Zach's buckskin shirt. If he was going to save himself, now was the time. Another thirty seconds and it would be over. He saw bloodlust gleaming in Erskine's eyes. Bloodlust, and triumph. But the whites had a saying: Never put the cart before the horse. The man hadn't won yet.

Zach suddenly released the Hawken and lanced his forefingers into Erskine's eyes. His nails scraped deep. Erskine bellowed and pushed away, blinking frantically to try to restore his vision. The tension went out of Erskine's knife arm. Instantly, Zach grasped it with his other hand. Then, coiling his shoulder muscles, he forced Erskine's right forearm up and in, sinking the steel into Erskine's own throat.

Scrambling backward, Zach snatched the Hawken and stood. Everyone was gaping at Erskine, who had foolishly ripped the blade out and was now attempting in vain to staunch the river of blood pouring from the cavity. Convulsions erupted, the big man flopping like a fish out of water, sputtering and gasping the whole while. It was soon over. The convulsions lessened, the sputtering tapered. Erskine went limp, mouth agape. A spreading pool formed.

"You killed him!" Sylvia Banner exclaimed, aghast.

Zach pivoted. What else did she expect? Titus, Zach noticed, had undone only one of the knots. "You'll be next if you don't finish!" he warned, thumbing back the Hawken's hammer. At the loud click, Titus stiffened. Lou was still doubled over, still breathing hard.

Louisa couldn't help herself. Her stomach, still sore from Erskine's punches when she was first caught, had flared with exquisite agony when he hit her again. She'd brought it on herself. Dread of being drugged and raped had spurred her into slamming her legs against Erskine's shins, and in retaliation he had held her down and driven his fist into her abdomen.

Only now was Lou regaining her senses. She'd heard Zach's voice and tried to straighten, but her head was swimming so badly she felt nauseous. She saw thick fingers pick at the loops around her ankles. As the rope fell, she slowly unfurled and beheld Erskine, dead. "Good riddance," she said bitterly. "I just regret it wasn't me who did him in, like I did that Coyfield."

Sylvia Banner looked at her. "You've *killed* before?"

"When I've had to," Lou answered. The last time had been when a bunch of hill folk from Arkansas tried to wipe out the King family.

"But you're just a snip of a girl," Banner said.

Titus was fumbling at the rope around Lou's wrists. She smiled at her beloved, wanting to throw her arms around him. Beyond Zach was an old-timer she had never seen before. Over by the van, another man was holding a bloody hand to his side. The driver had his arms in the air and was wisely standing stock-still.

"I was worried sick," Zach said, a lump forming in his throat as waves of affection rippled through him. It required considerable effort to focus on the matter at hand. There would be time enough later to tell her exactly how worried he had been, and how glad he was to have her safe and sound.

"You and me both," Lou replied.

Titus unraveled the last knot and threw the rope down. "I'm sorry about Erskine hurting you."

"I know you are," Lou said. "Take my advice and find a new line of work. As for you . . ." Lou turned toward Sylvia Banner. "This is for what you did to me." Her fist caught the brunette square on the jaw. Banner tottered rearward as if drunk, her hands flailing for support that wasn't there. "And this is for what you did to all those other poor girls." Again Lou swung, a solid right that sent Banner stumbling against the van.

"These are just for the hell of it." Lou hit Sylvia again and again, in the face, in the stomach. Compelled by red-hot fury, she boxed the woman's ear, smashed her on the nose, split her upper and lower lip. Not once did Banner try to defend herself. Groaning, she slumped to the ground, stunned. Lou would have hit her some more had Zach not spoken.

"Move out of the way and I'll shoot her."

Breathing heavily, Lou shook her head. "No. We can't."

"We must," Zach said. "All of them deserve to die." They were enemies, were they not? And first and foremost, he was a Shoshone warrior.

Lou stepped back, placing a hand on the barrel of his rifle. "No," she insisted. She didn't care about the others, but Titus had treated her decently enough, and he had a family.

"Your fiancée is right, son," George Milhouse said. "Murder a white woman and an army of whites will be after your hide. They'll tear this city apart to find you. Much as I hate to say it, we should let Banner live."

Zach boiled with rage that demanded release. "What about this one?" He leveled the rifle at the driver. "And the one who tried to shoot me."

Milhouse came up beside him. "They're scum, I grant you. If anyone deserves to be rubbed out, they do. But the shots are bound to be heard. And keep in mind that whoever is runnin' this operation is going to be mad enough as it is at losin' your gal."

"He's going to lose more than her," Zach stated. Shoving the Hawken into Lou's hands, he climbed in the van.

Light spilling from the building's open door into the van revealed five young women, bound and seated on long benches on either side. They had heard what transpired. A blonde nervously slid toward him, asking, "Are you fixing to free us, Injun? For real?"

Zach let his Bowie answer her. One by one he freed them all. Several drew back at his touch, whether in fear or disgust, Zach couldn't say. When he was done, they looked at one another in amazement.

The blonde rose. "This is awful white of you, Injun."

She meant it as a compliment. It was a standard figure of speech on the frontier. But it angered Zach, because it implied only whites had noble sentiments. "No, it is awful Shoshone of me. Remember this the next time you hear someone say the only good Indian is a dead one."

"I will," the young woman promised. With that, she was gone, bolting like a doe, and on her heels fled the others, jostling one another in their haste to get out the narrow doorway.

Lou hadn't realized the van contained other captives. She smiled as Zach emerged, sheathing his Bowie. "That's five more lives you've saved tonight, Stalking Coyote," she said proudly.

Sylvia Banner had sat up, her back propped against a front wheel. "Gloat while you can, you little witch. He won't be able to save your skin or his once Lon hears about this. None of you are long for this world."

Zach almost kicked her in the teeth. The fact she was a woman was of no consequence. An enemy was an enemy. She had brought suffering to the one he loved. Backing away from the driver and Titus, he reclaimed his rifle, then clasped Louisa's hand. "Do not attempt to follow us. Any of you."

"It won't be us who blows out your wick," Banner said. "The man who runs this operation will send a pack of hired killers to do the job. You won't stand a prayer."

"They'll never find us," Zach said. "Not in a city this size."

Banner touched a finger to her bloody lips. "Don't kid yourself, savage. Maybe you'll run off to the mountains to save your skin, but that won't help you. And in the meantime we have Milhouse."

"How do you mean?"

"The old man has nowhere to go, nowhere he can hide. George can hole up in his store if he wants, but they'll just burn it to the ground with him inside."

"If they try, they will answer to me," Zach vowed.

Banner uttered a brittle laugh. "Idiot. Do you expect Lon Festerman to quake in his boots because an upstart savage threatens him?"

Lou did not like the look on Zach's face. She pulled him toward the alley, saying, "Ignore her. She's just mad. This will be the end of it, I'm sure."

More laughter pealed as they retreated around the corner, George Milhouse hobbling rapidly to keep up. Zach checked the street before crossing, then swiveled and didn't take his eyes off the mouth of the alley until they were in the Trapper's Haven. Barring the door, he turned, and was nearly knocked off his feet by his sweetheart.

"Oh, Stalking Coyote! For a while I thought I'd never see you again!" Lou gave rein to her joy. She hugged him, lavishing kisses on his cheeks and lips, forgetting they weren't alone until a chair scraped. Composing herself, she wrapped her left arm around Zach's waist and turned.

"I reckon you young'uns should light a shuck while you can," George Milhouse said. "It'll be a spell before anyone comes after us."

Zach placed a hand on a pistol. "You stuck by me when Lou was in trouble. We'll stick by you now."

The trapper leaned his walking stick against the stove. "I admire any coon with grit, and you've got more than most, boy. But you've got your filly to think of. She was lucky this time. If she falls into their clutches again, they'll do things to her no gentleman can talk about in mixed company."

Louisa knew nothing about the old man other than that he had risked his life to save hers. That alone was enough to earn him her undying gratitude and respect. "Why don't you come with us?" she suggested. "I have relatives who can help."

"Are these kin of yours mountaineers?" Milhouse asked hopefully. "A handful of mountain men are worth a hundred city fellers."

"They're visiting from Ohio. Uncle Earnest is a lawyer, and Uncle Thomas works at the mill."

"Fat lot of good they'll do, unless your uncle Earnest beats Festerman to death with his law books."

58

"We don't need them," Zach interjected. "We don't need anyone. This is our problem, and we'll settle it ourselves." He detached himself from Lou and squatted in front of Milhouse. "I want to know all there is to learn about this Lon Festerman."

"Why? What do you have in mind?"

Zach gazed from Milhouse to Lou and back again. "There is only one way to end this. We must kill him before he kills us."

Chapter Five

Half an hour later a shadow detached itself from the front of the Trapper's Haven and glided into the alley beside the dress shop. Zachary King, Bowie knife in hand, came to the yard at the rear.

His Hawken was with Lou. Persuading her to stay with Milhouse had been a challenge, but it was for the best. She would object if she knew what he planned to do. He had told her he was going to find out where their horses were, which wasn't the whole truth.

The yard was empty except for Erskine's body, which lay where it had fallen. The van had clattered off a while ago, Horace lashing the team in a frenzy and casting a menacing glare at the trapper's shop. Were it up to Zach, he'd have shot Horace from the seat, but George Milhouse protested it would cause too much of a stir. As the oldster had put it, "Firing a gun in the city limits is the one thing our peerless constables won't allow. Even for duelin'. Which is why all duels are now held on Bloody Island, out on the Mississippi. So long as a person commits murder quietly, the constables don't much mind. Unless it's one of the city's bigwigs."

Lon Festerman qualified. According to Milhouse, Festerman was one of the leading citizens. A wealthy man whose ill-gotten riches were reaped in the flesh trade, Festerman peddled young women like ordinary merchants peddled pots and pans. He sold their bodies to anyone with enough money to afford an hour of their time.

Zach had heard about the white practice of prostitution from friends of his father. Mountaineers who returned from trips east bragged of their exploits. But it had always struck him as despicable, as showing an utter lack of respect for women.

Once, Zach had asked his pa why any woman would do such a thing: Why would they let strange men paw them for money? "Believe it or not," his pa had said, "some women like to. Others are forced into selling themselves. They're broke and have nowhere else to turn. What it boils down to is money. A woman can earn a lot in a short amount of time, more than they can at any other job." *The whites and their money!* Zach thought.

Among Indian tribes the practice was rarely indulged. Some tribes, in fact, were noted for the purity of their women. Cheyenne maidens wore rope chastity belts so they would be untouched when they took a mate. Among the Apaches and a few others, any woman who prostituted herself was punished by being mutilated, by having her nose cut off, or an ear.

Prostitution among the Shoshones was unheard of. Married women were expected to be loyal to their husbands. Unmarried maidens were allowed to do as they pleased. But since few warriors wanted to take as their wife any woman who had a reputation for sharing herself with every male in the tribe, maidens tended to stay maidens until they shared a lodge with their husband.

The Crows were different. A Crow warrior might offer his wife to a visiting white for a night in exchange for trade goods, and saw nothing wrong in doing so. But then, the

Crows and the Shoshones did not see eye to eye on many things. Bitter enemies, they routinely raided one another. So low was the Shoshone opinion of Crows that one of the worst insults a Shoshone could inflict was to say another Shoshone was "just like a Crow."

Zach had counted coup on Crows, as well as Piegans, Bloods, and Sioux. He had counted coup on whites, too, and was about to do so again. Stealthily moving toward the rear door, he pressed an ear to it. All seemed quiet. He tested and found the door unlocked. Opening it a crack, he gazed into an empty room that contained a table, chairs, and a cot. On his left was another door, partly ajar.

Slipping inside, Zach heard voices. He crept up behind the other door. A man was talking.

". . . much like the notion of leaving you alone, Miss Banner."

"I'll be fine, Titus," Sylvia Banner said. "Odds are, those three have hightailed it. If not, they wouldn't be stupid enough to hurt me. And someone has to be here when Lon's boys arrive."

"I still don't like it," Titus said.

"Do as I say. Go to the livery and get their horses."

"You really want me to buy them back? Garcia will think we're crazy. You just sold that dun and the mare to him earlier today."

"For him to dispose of as he sees fit, yes. But we've done Garcia many favors in the past. Now I need one in return. We must have both horses, both saddles, and everything else the savage and the girl own." Banner paused. "I just hope he hasn't gotten rid of everything already."

"Why is it so important?"

"Think, Titus, think. Lon might send some of the constables on his payroll. To make it look legal, they'll need proof the savage murdered Erskine. And what better proof than the savage's own horse, found at the scene?"

"Oh. I get it."

"Good. Now, off you go. Don't dally. It shouldn't take you more than fifteen minutes. If Garcia gripes, tell him he can explain to Lon Festerman personally tomorrow. There's nothing like a good threat to motivate people."

The front door opened and closed. Zach sidled to the jamb. Sylvia Banner was staring out the window, watching Titus depart. When she turned, she wore a twisted smile made more so by her swollen lips and puffy cheek. Walking down an aisle to a cabinet, she opened it and removed a bottle of liquor and a tall glass. "I can't wait to spit on that savage's corpse," she remarked.

As noiseless as a mountain lion, Zach stalked to within arm's reach of her. Banner tilted her head and swallowed. Sighing, she rotated. Shock riveted her in place and she dropped the glass, which shattered at her feet.

"You!"

"Me."

Banner glanced at the Bowie and blanched. Recovering her composure, she snapped, "What brings you back so soon, bastard?"

"I came for our horses," Zach said. That wasn't all he had come for, but she didn't need to know that just yet.

"You're wasting your time. I don't know where they are."

Zach held the knife low, at waist level. "Yet another lie. Among my people it is said that someone who lies speaks with two tongues. You speak with ten."

"This from a filthy savage?" Banner laughed. "Ever hear of a kettle calling the pot black?"

What she was implying wasn't lost on Zach. "Because I'm part Indian, I must be as big a liar as you? Is that it?"

The wicked smile curled her lips again. "You're smarter than I gave you credit for. So do the smart thing and leave."

"I'm staying until our horses show up."

"So you heard, did you?" Banner gestured. "Suit yourself. You're digging your own grave. Lon Festerman will have ten of his men here within the hour. Maybe some constables, too. They'll bury you, 'breed. You and that hussy who wants you for a husband."

It took all of Zach's self-control not to slash her from

chin to navel. As it was, he took a half-step, the Bowie poised to thrust, and something in his expression caused Banner to recoil against the cabinet.

"Harm me and you'll have every white man in the city after you!"

"Will I? If they find out what you have been doing to young white girls?"

"Never happen," Banner retorted. "You have no proof unless you count your fiancée. And no one is going to take her word over mine. I'm a respected businesswoman. Louisa is a little tart. A girl willing to give herself to an *Indian*."

Zach's knuckles were white, but he held the Bowie still. "People like you make me wish I had no white blood. The world would be better off without you." He had said it plainly. But she, unlike him, missed the significance.

"You're a fine one to talk. How many whites have lost their lives to savages like you? One of these days we'll exterminate every last Indian! This land will be safe for decent folks."

"Decent?" Zach practically spat the word. "Was it decent of the whites to drive so many eastern tribes from their land? Was it decent of the whites to wipe out whole villages with smallpox and other disease?"

"Listen to you. Who are you to sit in judgment on us? We can't be blamed for making Indians sick. Sickness just happens. And as for taking over Indian land, the strong always push out the weak."

For years Zach had listened to whites say the same thing. For years he had been the victim of their bile and their pride. Now all his resentment surfaced, and he quivered from the intensity of his emotion. "When the whites try to push west of the Mississippi they will learn just how strong the red man is. The Plains and mountain tribes will not sit still for it. Much blood will be spilled, much of it white."

"Big talk, savage. Just what I'd expect. But you're missing an important point—on purpose, I'll bet."

"What point?"

GET YOUR 4
FREE* BOOKS NOW—
A VALUE BETWEEN
$16 AND $20

Mail the Free* Book Certificate Today!

FREE* BOOKS
CERTIFICATE!

YES! I want to subscribe to the Leisure Western Book Club. Please send me my 4 FREE* BOOKS. Then, each month, I'll receive the four newest Leisure Western Selections to preview FREE* for 10 days. If I decide to keep them, I will pay the Special Member's Only discounted price of just $3.36 each, a total of $13.44 ($14.50 US in Canada). This saves me between $3 and $6 off the bookstore price. There are no shipping, handling or other charges.* There is no minimum number of books I must buy and I may cancel the program at any time. In any case, the 4 FREE* BOOKS are mine to keep—at a value of between $17 and $20!

*In Canada, add $5.00 Canadian shipping and handling per order for first shipment. For all subsequent shipments to Canada the cost of membership in the Book Club is $14.50 US, which includes $7.50 shipping and handling per month. All payments must be made in US currency.

Name _____

Address _____

City_____ State_____ Country_____

Zip_____ Telephone_____

If under 18, parent or guardian must sign. Terms, prices and conditions subject to change. Subscription subject to acceptance. Leisure Books reserves the right to reject any order or cancel any subscription.

Tear here and mail your FREE* book card today!

"Don't Indians make war on other Indians? I've heard the Pawnees are always fighting the Sioux, the Comanches fighting the Arapahos, the Blackfeet always out to scalp anyone and everyone. So how can you stand there and blame whites for making war on your kind when Indians make war on one another?"

"Indians fight to defend their territory. Whites only want to wipe us out."

"Who are you kidding? A lot of Indians want to see all white men dead, too."

Zach felt himself weakening. He had to remember that the real issue wasn't how the red man and the white man treated each other. This was between the woman and him, personally. "You hurt the one I love."

Sylvia Banner studied him. "What does that have to do with what we were just talking about? Do you think I did it because of you? Hell, 'breed, I picked her because she said no one knew she was in St. Louis. She could disappear and it wouldn't cause a stir."

"Your men beat her."

"They only did what they had to in order to subdue her." Banner shifted toward the cabinet, freezing when he hiked the knife a few inches. "I just want another drink. Is that all right?"

Zach nodded. He would permit her a last treat. Then a twinge of guilt pricked him, and he said, "Tell me something. If Lou and I were to leave St. Louis right this minute, if we rode out promising never to come back, would that be the end of it?"

"Hardly. Lon Festerman won't rest until he's tracked you down. Oh, you'd probably escape to the mountains. But if you ever came back and he found out, well, let's just say Lon has a long memory." Banner removed the bottle and another glass. "In any event, your friend Milhouse is as good as dead."

"Could you talk Festerman into letting us be?"

"No, even if I wanted to. Which I don't." Banner raised

the bottle, touching it to a bruise on her right cheek. "Look at what your girl did to me! Were it up to me, I'd have her gutted like a fish. When Lon gets hold of her, I'll still do everything I can to make her life miserable."

Without being aware of it, the brunette had sealed her fate. Zach felt an icy calm grip him, the same icy calm that seized him in the heat of battle. "What if I ask you to forget what happened?"

"I swear. You're as dumb as your girlfriend." Banner filled the glass and placed the bottle back in the cabinet. "I'm tired of wasting breath on you. Get out of here while you still can."

"Not yet. There is something I came to do."

Banner still didn't comprehend. "Oh. The horses. They should be here any minute. Take them, and good riddance. You'll never escape Lon Festerman."

"I don't intend to try."

Sipping, Banner winced as the alcohol made contact with her split lips. "Hasn't it sunk in that you don't stand a prayer against him? Save Lon the trouble and put a ball in your own head."

"I'm going to make wolf meat of him."

About to take another sip, Banner grinned. "All by yourself? Oh, I forgot. You've got that old buzzard and your snip of a fiancée to help."

"Festerman is my enemy."

"I'll let him know. He'll be terrified."

"You are my enemy."

Banner chuckled. "I'm quaking." She motioned at the door. "Go out back and wait for Titus."

Zach couldn't understand why she hadn't guessed yet. Maybe it was because she was confident he wouldn't dare incur the wrath of every white in St. Louis by harming her. Or maybe it was because he was a 'breed, and many whites naturally thought they were superior to anyone with red skin. But he wanted her to know what was coming. He wanted her to feel the same terror Louisa had felt. "You are a threat to the one I love."

Banner was lifting the glass. "I'm not half the threat Lon

Festerman is. Haven't you got that through your thick skull?"

"But finding him will be harder than it was finding you. So I will kill him next."

"Next?" Sylvia Banner turned to marble. Zach saw insight flare at last, saw it swell and then be submerged. "You can't be saying what I think you're saying. Indians and half-breeds can't so much as lay a finger on a white woman. You'd never get away with it."

"Maybe. But it is more important to protect Lou." Zach held the Bowie so light gleamed brightly on the blade. "One cut is all it will take."

Fear resurfaced in Banner, building rapidly to raw terror. She backed into the cabinet, her eyes saucers. "Think about what you're doing! Hurt me and you won't be the only one who pays. Your girl might end up in prison."

"For what? This is my idea, not hers."

Sylvia looked toward the entrance, then at the door in the left wall. "Haven't you ever heard of an accessory to a crime? The court will blame her because she's your woman and she's had a part in all this."

Zach was unsure whether Banner was telling the truth. The law sounded silly enough to be one the whites lived by. But it was of no consequence. "If we are caught, I'll admit to what I did. I will accept all of the blame."

"That still might not help her." Banner began to slide along the wall, toward the door into the other room. "So be smart. Don't do anything rash. To show my gratitude, I'll give back yours horses without any fuss. How would that be?"

The time for conversation was over. Zach paced her, just out of reach, waiting for her to break and bolt.

His silence unnerved her more. "Now, you hold on, 'breed! I'm walking out of here, and if you know what's good for you, you won't interfere. Don't lift a finger against me. Not if you value your girl's life."

"It is *because* I value her life that I can't let you leave." Zach was in no hurry. The fear she was feeling repaid her for the fear she had caused Lou.

"But I'm a *woman*!"

"Female rattlesnakes are as deadly as the male. She-bears even more dangerous than male grizzlies."

Banner was ten feet from the door now, and moving faster. "But I'm a human being, not a damn animal!"

"Isn't that what I am?" Zach asked.

"I don't follow you."

"You call me a savage. You call me a 'breed. To you, I am less than a human being. To you, I am an animal. Isn't that so?"

"No, no, no," Banner said, trembling now, trembling so badly she sloshed some of the scotch onto her hand. "I never said any such thing. You're putting words in my mouth to excuse murder."

"How do you excuse selling women to Festerman? What do you tell yourself late at night so you can sleep?"

"I do it for the money. Ask your fiancée."

"With Indians it is whiskey."

"How's that?" Banner wasn't really listening. She was close now, and she stopped to gird herself.

"Money is your weakness," Zach said. "With Indians it is whiskey. The white man's fool water, it's called. Some can't live without it."

Banner looked at the half-full glass in her hand as if contemplating whether to finish it.

"I don't drink. I don't have a hankering for a lot of money. But I do want to spend the rest of my life with Louisa May Clark, and I won't let anyone or anything spoil that." Zach had said all that needed saying. "Are you ready to meet your Maker?"

"No!"

Sylvia Banner swept her arm up. The alcohol splashed Zach in the face, stinging his eyes and getting into his nose and mouth. For a moment he couldn't see. He heard the door flung open as he swiped at himself with a sleeve. Banner was just racing through the doorway.

Zach gave chase. The brunette angled past the table to gain the outside door. She'd have made it, too, had she not glanced back and accidentally collided with one of the chairs. Her legs were knocked out from under her and she toppled, taking the chair down with her.

Raising the knife, Zach moved in to end it. Banner was entangled, but she didn't stay that way for long. Flinging her legs out, she sent the chair hurtling at him. He dodged to the left, but a chair leg clipped him on the right elbow, jarring a nerve, and his arm went completely numb.

Sylvia Banner scrambled toward the door. Zach executed a leaping dive to stop her and succeeded in wrapping his left hand around her ankle. She cried out, then began kicking him on the head and shoulder with her other foot. Zach tried to use his right arm to block her blows, but it would barely move. It was tingling something awful, hurting almost as bad.

"You're not murdering me, you filthy savage!" Banner snarled, slamming her heel into his temple.

Dazed, Zach felt his grip loosen. Banner pushed upright, but she only took a single step before he flung himself forward and bowled her over. He ended up on top of her legs. Banner screeched, raking him with her long fingernails. They bit into his neck, into his cheek. Then she speared her fingers at his eyes.

Zach rolled off her to avoid being blinded. His right arm could move a few inches, but that was all. Switching the Bowie from his right hand to his left, he sprang anew, reaching Banner as she grabbed for the latch. Some instinct made her spin away at the instant he slashed at her arm. He missed, but now he was between her and the door.

Banner attempted to dart past him, but all Zach had to do was pivot on the balls of his feet. Breathing heavily, she slowly backed off. Her hair was disheveled, her dress torn above the hem.

"May you rot in hell!"

"If I do, I will see you there," Zach countered, then lunged, seeking to transfix her. Banner sped around the table, gripped it by the edge, and heaved with all her strength. Zach danced backward to avoid it.

The brunette did the last thing he expected. She turned on her heel and flew into the dress shop.

She was heading for the front door! Zach sprinted after her. If Banner reached the street, she might find help. Passersby were few at that time of night, but people did come by now and then—mainly men returning home after indulging at their favorite tavern or grop shop. Yet they weren't Zach's biggest concern. Lou might spot her. And sweet, misguided Lou wouldn't let him do what was best for all of them.

Such were Zach's thoughts as he charged into the shop. Better for him if he had not let his mind stray, because when he came through the doorway Sylvia Banner was waiting for him, holding an unlit lantern. She swung, hard, crashing it against his head. Glass shattered into a hundred shards, and Zach was sent staggering into a dress rack. He couldn't keep his balance. Down he went, the rack and two dozen dresses on top of him.

"Try to kill me, will you?" Banner declared, swinging again and again.

His arm still defying his will, Zach clutched several dresses and threw them at her to buy the precious seconds it would take for him to stand. But Banner swatted them aside.

Zach's plan to inspire terror in her had gone terribly awry. She was no longer scared. She was *mad*. Fiery mad. So mad, she didn't seem to care what happened to her as long as she could inflict an injury, or worse.

"I'll have your eyes cut out for a keepsake, half-breed!"

Zach ducked under the lantern. Flashing his good arm at her, he cut Banner across the hand. Not deep, but deep enough for her to yelp and drop the lantern as if it were a hot coal. Rotating, she moved toward the entrance. But Zach was too quick for her. Still partly covered with garments, he shoved upward and tackled her.

They tumbled, bringing more racks down. Clothes piled on top. Zach sought to throw them off without losing his grip on Banner, but it was impossible. She struggled like a caught snake, wriggling and sliding and doing everything in her power to thwart him.

"Nooooo! It can't end like this! It can't!"

Zach stabbed at where he believed her chest to be, but the Bowie sheared into loose dresses. Banner's infernal nails sliced into his neck again, so close to his jugular that he instinctively jerked away, allowing her to raise herself onto her knees. He struck lower, but she avoided him.

Flustered, Zach pumped erect. He had underestimated her. He'd assumed slaying her would be easy, but the woman fought with the ferocity of a mountain lion. Now she was heading for the front door again. To intercept her, he veered around a rack. She stopped short, clenching and unclenching her fists.

"If only I had a gun!"

Zach had two, but he couldn't use either. Shots were bound to be heard by Lou. He edged forward, the tingling in his right arm fading. Banner had been lucky so far, but no one's luck lasted forever.

Suddenly she pivoted and ran toward the other room. Zach pursued her, but the fallen racks slowed him down. As she raced through the doorway she yelled something he couldn't quite make out. He crossed the threshold and halted.

Titus was back. He stood just inside the outside door, Sylvia Banner behind him, clinging to his broad shoulders. The big man looked at the overturned furniture, then at his employer, and finally at Zach. "What's going on here?"

Banner was gasping for breath. "What do you think is going on, you cretin? That savage is trying to kill me! You've got to stop him!"

Crouching, Zach waited for the man to rush him. But Titus stayed where he was.

"I can't let you hurt Miss Banner. I'm sorry, mister. I know you're Lou's fella, and she's real nice, but I'll stop you if I can."

Zach had a decision to make. His urge to kill warred with Lou's last words, right before he left to get the horses. "Don't kill anyone else. Especially don't lay a finger on Titus. He treated me decently, and I like him." Zach was in a quandary. Should he slay them both, against his beloved's wishes, and be done with it? Or let them live, possibly to endanger Lou later?

"So what's it going to be?" Titus asked.

Chapter Six

Louisa May Clark was glad to have her mare back, but not so glad about the prospect of tangling with Lon Festerman. The old trapper claimed it was necessary, but Lou couldn't stop trying to come up with another way of settling it. "Maybe if Zach talked to him," she had proposed while they were waiting for her betrothed to return from the dress shop.

"Lay him down in front of a runaway freight wagon, why don't you?" George Milhouse had responded. "You'd get the same result. Festerman will have him butchered on sight." The trapper had warmly clasped her hand. "Zach has the right idea. It's us or that buzzard, and I'd rather it was the buzzard."

Maybe so, but Lou was afraid. Not for herself, for Zach. He could be hotheaded at times, to say nothing of his stubborn streak. Now that he had set himself to killing Lon Festerman, Zach wouldn't rest until the deed was done, until he had put a lead ball into Festerman's wicked heart. But lead balls weren't particular about whom they brought low. It might well be that Zach was the one who would die, felled by a shot fired by one of Lon Festerman's men or Festerman himself.

It didn't help Lou's anxiety any that Zach had come back from the dress shop in a surly mood. He didn't volunteer why, and she didn't ask.

Behind the Trapper's Haven was a small pen in which George Milhouse kept a gelding that looked to be almost as old as he was. Zach had offered to help throw a saddle on it, but the trapper refused. He'd rather do it himself.

Now the three of them were winding along the city's gloomy and often narrow byways. By Lou's reckoning it was past two in the morning. Few people were abroad, or had been when they started out. But the farther they went, the deeper into the dark heart of the city they traveled, the more they saw.

The old trapper guided them, stopping frequently to get his bearings. When Lou asked why he was having such a hard time, he mustered a lopsided grin. "It's been a spell since I roamed these parts, girl. I don't care to make a mistake and end up in Kentucky."

Zach stared at a pair of men in city clothes who were weaving down the street, both singing a lusty ballad. Rutting elk made more pleasant sounds. "How much longer?" he inquired.

"Less than an hour" was Milhouse's guess.

Presently they came to a junction, one of many lacking signs to identify which street was which. The trapper reined up and scratched his chin awhile. "If I recollect correctly, one of these will take us down to the bawdy house we're huntin' for."

"We are?" Lou said. No one had mentioned to her anything about visiting a house of ill repute. "I thought you knew right where Festerman lives."

"The general area," Milhouse said. "In one of about sixty mansions. We could go door to door, if that's what you want. Shouldn't take more than a month of Sundays. Or we can ask at the fanciest den of iniquity he owns."

"It'll be open this late?"

Milhouse found the question amusing. "Nighttime is when folks do stuff they're too afraid to do in broad daylight for fear of being caught. Bawdy houses do their best business after the sun goes down. They usually stay open until dawn."

Lou had never been in one before, but she had been curious about the goings-on since she first heard about them when she was ten or twelve. Asking her parents had been out of the question. Her mother, bless her soul, held no truck with fallen doves. And her father thought it sinful to even mention the word "bawdy." It had been her cousins on her father's side, Uncle Thomas's girls, Ethel and Gladys, who liked to speculate about things decent girls weren't supposed to. Especially Ethel, the oldest, who always had a naughty streak and brought her ma and pa no end of misery from her shenanigans.

More and more pedestrians appeared. Men and women, many arm in arm. Carriages became common. So did streetlamps.

Zach hadn't seen much of St. Louis after sunset on his previous visit. Being a small boy at the time had a lot to do with it; his ma had made him go to bed by eight. So when Milhouse turned into another street lit from end to end and crammed with a flowing stream of humanity, Zach was dazzled. So much activity at so late an hour. He wouldn't admit as much, but the boundless energy of his father's people never failed to amaze him. Whites were always on the go, always doing this or that. Most couldn't stand to sit still for more than two minutes. They thrived on keeping busy. On chaos.

In comparison, Shoshones valued peace and tranquillity above all else. Yes, the warriors liked to go on raids and count coup, but village life was by and large a quiet existence, where order and harmony were valued above all else.

Many a day Zach had wondered how it was the whites and Indians were so different. In many respects they were utter opposites. Was it because of the blood in their veins, or the manner in which they were brought up? He'd asked his pa once, but all his father would say was, "What people have in common is more important than what sets them apart."

His father was like that. Always looking for the best in people. Always willing to lend a helping hand, to give others the benefit of the doubt. A number of times his pa's trusting nature had nearly gotten them wiped out. Zach still vividly remembered when his father saved two New Yorkers from hostiles and brought them home to recover. They recovered, all right, and then tried to slaughter the family.

Zach had been alone with his baby sister when one of them tried to break into the cabin. It was the scariest night of his young life, but it taught him an important lesson. He should never, ever trust anyone until they showed they were worthy of it. Or, as the mountaineers liked to say, "Keep an open mind, but keep your gun handy."

George Milhouse was slanting toward a hitch rail. "We're walking from here on out?" Zach asked, uneasy at mingling with the throng.

"There's the place we want," the trapper said.

He referred to a three-story building, painted yellow and garishly lit, like a land-bound steamboat. On balconies overlooking the street, attractive women in tight dresses paraded and called down to likely customers to entice them inside.

Zach dismounted and tied the dun. He was braced for unfriendly looks and insults, but no one gave him a second glance. Here he was, a half-breed adrift in a sea of whites, and it merited no interest. A closer scrutiny revealed why.

St. Louis was a boiling pot, a city where men from different countries and different cultures freely mixed. Spaniards, Frenchmen, Americans, Indians, they were all there, and not one was trying to kill the other.

It amazed Zach, for never in a million years would the Blackfeet, the Crows, the Sioux, and the Utes do the same. They had been at war too long to ever bury the lance. Once again, the whites were different. Not all that long ago America and France had been at war, and France and Spain had also been in conflict. Yet here they were, men of different nationalities, treating each other as friendly as you please.

Lou glued herself to her sweetheart's elbow. She was surprised to find herself feeling frightened by the swirling press of countless people. Yet this was just what she had looked forward to on the long ride across the prairie. To being back in civilization. To the thrill of city life. She blamed her nervousness on her ordeal at the dress shop. What else could it be?

George Milhouse shouldered toward the yellow building. "I'd recommend the two of you stay outside. I'm an old hand at this. It shouldn't take long."

"We'd better stick together," Zach said. He'd learned his lesson with Lou. Until he counted coup on Lon Festerman, he wasn't letting the trapper out of his sight.

Milhouse had to raise his voice to be heard. "You'd both attract too much attention. Surely you don't want them to notice your gal, do you?"

"They won't lay a finger on her."

"Is that so? Need I remind you that you're only one person? Festerman has enough cutthroats on his payroll to start a small war."

A short flight of steps brought them to a wide porch where more painted women paraded. Milhouse stopped and grasped Zach's wrist. "Listen to me, son. Please. Wait here."

Zach refused to give in. He was confident they could pull it off. Then the gaudy glass doors opened and a pair of hawk-faced men armed with a brace of pistols stepped out, broad shoulder to broad shoulder. They rooted themselves, the powerfully built one on the right extending his palm.

"Hold it right there, gramps. Where do you three misfits think you're going?"

George Milhouse chortled and wagged his walking stick. "I'm treatin' myself to a night on the town. At my age I don't get the hankerin' very often, so I'd be obliged if you'd step aside before the urge passes."

Neither man moved. "What about them?" demanded the one on the right, indicating Zach and Louisa.

"What about 'em? They're with me."

"Think again, gramps. No Indians allowed."

"Who says so?"

"Can't you read?" The man pointed at a large sign on the wall.

Lou had already seen it. The establishment was known as The Gilded Lily. Patrons were required to behave like gentlemen. No chewing tobacco was allowed on the premises. No spitting on the floors, no striking the ladies, no rowdy behavior. And in bold letters at the bottom NO BLACKS, INDIANS OR DOGS PERMITTED INSIDE.

Milhouse's lips moved as he read. When he was done, he declared, "Tarnation, mister! My friend here isn't an Indian. He's half white."

"If you say so," the man responded. "But he looks like a redskin. So he doesn't get to go in."

Zach would have torn into both of them, but Lou placed a restraining hand on his arm.

"There's a place down the street called Lowe's. It caters to blacks and 'breeds," the man said.

Milhouse thoughtfully plucked at his beard. "But I can still go in, can't I?"

"Sure. You're white enough. Have fun, old man. Ask for Happy Harriet. She likes to frolic under the sheets with wrinkled coots like you. Claims it's less wear and tear."

Laughing, the pair went back inside, taking up posts on either side of the entrance. Milhouse laughed, too, but as soon as the doors swung shut, he turned to Zach and

Lou. "Damned upstarts! There was a time when I'd have bashed in both their noggins without breathin' hard." Curling a finger, he moved to one side. "We're not licked. I'll find out what we need to know. You two stick close."

"How long will you be?" Zach asked.

The trapper smirked. "I can't rightly say. It depends on Happy Harriet. I might need to poke around a bit." Milhouse chucked. "Get it? Poke around a bit? I sure am a caution sometimes."

"You mean ask questions?" Lou said.

Milhouse looked at her, then at Zach, and sighed. "Downright pitiful. Why, when I was your age, I—" Catching himself, he hobbled toward the glass doors. "Just do me a favor. Try to stay out of trouble while I'm gone. Find a nice, quiet spot to wait." One of the men opened a door for him, and he plastered a smile on his face. "Why, thank you, sir! Now, can you direct me to the dove you mentioned? She's in for the treat of her life."

"I don't like this," Zach said, watching as the trapper was led across a plush parlor toward a cluster of waiting lovelies. Any delays were unacceptable. They had to track down Festerman before Festerman tracked them down.

"Mr. Milhouse knows what's best," Lou said, clasping his hand. "Let's stick close to the horses. We don't want them stolen again."

At the end of the bottom step nearest the hitch rail they sat to wait. Zach was in a funk and couldn't stop fidgeting. Nothing had gone right since they arrived in St. Louis, just as he'd known would happen. They'd have been better off staying in the Rockies. The wilderness could be treacherous at times, but nowhere near as treacherous as so-called civilization. He stared glumly at the flow of passersby, regarding all of them as potential enemies.

Lou was having second thoughts about their plan. Slaying Lon Festerman might put them in more trouble than they already were. She was all for forgetting the whole thing and going to find her relatives, but there was a fly in the ointment. They couldn't very well desert George Milhouse. The old man had put his life at risk on their account. They owed it to him to do what they could.

"I wish we'd never left home," Zach commented.

"And what about my aunt and uncles?" Lou said. "After all the bother they've gone to, was I supposed to ignore their letter?"

"You have me and my family," Zach said. "We're your kin now. You don't need anyone else."

"A person can't turn their back on their past. I bet you couldn't leave your ma and pa for good."

"Ma and Pa, no. But Evelyn . . ." Zach's younger sister had been a thorn in his side since he could remember. She delighted in taunting him, in making his life miserable. How someone who had been such a cute, cuddly baby could grow up to be such a holy terror was beyond him.

"You love her and you know it," Lou said. "Brothers and sisters always squabble. I never had a sibling, but my cousins were always at each other's throats when we were little. You should be thankful you have her."

"I'm thankful I don't have *two* sisters. One is bad enough. Any more, and I'd go live with the Shoshones." Zach always aimed to do that one day anyway. His dream had been to become a prominent warrior, one whose word in council was highly respected. But then Louisa came along. Now his dream was to have a cabin of their own, and to raise a family. Just like his pa had done. He laughed lightly.

"It's nice to see your mood is improving. What tickled your funny bone?"

"Remember that talk we had about how many children we wanted to have?"

"Sure. We agreed on five. Why?"

"If we have any girls, my sons will hate me."

Lou playfully hugged him, forgetting where they were.

She felt him stiffen and assumed he was embarrassed by her public display of affection. A low grunt in front of them proved her wrong.

"What's this, then? A white gal fondling an Injun? Don't hardly seem right to me, Abner."

"Sure don't, Will."

Rivermen, it was widely believed, were the bane of St. Louis. The rowdies and toughs who worked the steamboats and barges were a lusty, violent breed who treated the city as if it were their own. When they weren't working, they were drinking, and when they weren't guzzling ale and grog, they'd fight at the drop of a hat, or the small caps they favored. A long-standing resentment existed between rivermen and frontiersmen, largely because both refused to back down to anyone who looked at them crosswise. And now here were two of the ruffians of the waterways, spoiling for trouble.

Zach was already close to the snapping point. He had tolerated more abuse in the past few hours than he had his entire life. It would take much to set him off. But he dampened his temper and said, "Don't bother us."

Abner, whose hands and beetling brows were exceptionally hairy, nudged his friend. "Did you hear the Injun, Will? Bossing us around like he's the captain or something?"

Zach inhaled the strong stink of grog. The pair were unsteady on their feet, their eyes bloodshot. They would be comical if not for the daggers wedged under their belts and the glints in their eyes. They wanted to provoke him.

Will had a red nose and a mustache as thin as thread. "I've never much cottoned to Injuns. What should we do with him?"

"Beat him to death?" Abner said. Swaying like a reed in the wind, he stepped to the stairs. "You shouldn't paw white women, Injun."

Louisa was afraid. Not of the rivermen, but of what

Stalking Coyote might do to them. Rising, she smiled. "He and I are to be married. So please leave us be."

"Married?" Abner was shocked. "Hell, girl. You don't look old enough to tie the knot. Wait another four or five years before you ruin your life. And find a white man to wed."

"He's part white—" Lou began to explain.

"No!" Zach pushed upright. "Don't make excuses." He was sick and tired of being pushed around. To the rivermen he said, "Go. Now. While you still can."

Abner lowered a hand to the hilt of his dagger. "A heathen should know better than to sass his betters." He reached for Lou's wrist. "Come with us, girl. We know a nice young fellow who'd be just right for you."

A snarl was torn from Zach, rising from deep in the tortured wellspring of his being and bursting out like the snarl of a riled panther. He was on his tormentor before the man could so much as blink, ramming the Hawken into the riverman's midsection. As drunk as the pair were, he figured they would be easy to overpower. But rivermen deserved their reputation. They were as tough as alligators.

Abner gripped the barrel and uncoiled, driving the stock against Zach and propelling him against the stairs. Zach sought to wrest the Hawken free, but the other riverman pounced, pinning his arms.

"Stop it!" Lou cried. She tried to intervene, but Abner gave her a shove that sent her tottering into the pedestrians. Someone helped steady her amid shouts of, "Fight! Fight!" People were stopping to watch.

Zach lost his footing when his left leg snagged on the bottom step. He fell and Will released him. Landing on his back, he slammed a heel into Will's shin while simultaneously hauling on the Hawken. Abner wouldn't give it up, though, and delivered a vicious kick at Zach's crotch. It narrowly missed.

"Someone stop them!" Lou shouted. She attempted to reach Zach, but others, eager to witness the outcome, roughly shouldered her aside. A crowd was swiftly gathering. "Please help us!" she begged.

Zach rolled to the left and began to rise, but both rivermen were on him in a twinkling, battering him, raining hard punches. Pummeled, he stumbled to the rear and bumped into the ring of spectators. Several seized him, laughing merrily at his plight. They stripped him of the Hawken, then pushed him toward the rivermen amid a chorus of yells.

"Come on, boys! Beat the tar out of this whelp!"

"Stomp the red devil into the dirt!"

"Five dollars says the Indian won't last five minutes!"

Abner and Will were waiting. Abner had drawn his glittering dagger and was set to spring. His partner was circling to the left.

Zach sidestepped as the dagger sought his neck. In retaliation, his Bowie flicked out and Abner screeched like a wounded eagle.

"He cut me! The damn 'breed cut me!"

"I'll settle his hash," Will said. Unarmed, he advanced. Maybe he had no real desire to hurt Zach. Maybe he thought Zach wouldn't harm him if he didn't have a weapon. Or maybe he was so drunk, he plain forgot. Whichever, he, too, screeched when the Bowie opened his shoulder.

Some in the throng cackled. Others hollered encouragement to the rivermen. No one voiced support for Zach. Hoots of scorn were directed at him, along with a few choice comments concerning his parentage.

Abner and Will grew deadly serious. Will had his dagger out now, and with a nod at his friend, he triggered the next attempt to bring Zach down. They converged from opposite directions.

Zach spun back and forth, facing one and then the other. He was outnumbered, but the Bowie's blade was twice the length of theirs. As long as he could keep them at arm's length, they couldn't do him any real harm. Abner tried to skip in close to thrust into his chest, but a sweep of the

Bowie dissuaded him. Yet even as Zach pivoted toward Abner, Will attacked. Only Zach's lightning reflexes spared him. He pivoted, his blade striking the riverman's, deflecting it.

"What's the matter with you two?" an onlooker wondered. "He's just a boy! My mother could do better!"

Gruff mirth added to the insult. Abner and Will swapped glances, then renewed their assault, skipping in close at the selfsame moment, Abner slicing low, Will cutting high.

Zach couldn't block both, so he didn't try. He leaped into the air, tucking his knees to his chest to evade Abner. As he jumped, he countered Will's slash with a sideways swipe. The rivermen skittered backward, upset their ploy had failed.

Those in the swelling crowd were enjoying themselves. Everyone had a comment to make. Their jeers incited the two rivermen into another gambit. Abner suddenly unbuckled his belt and slid it off. The ruffian wrapped one end around his free hand, the big buckle dangling at his knees.

Puzzled as to what good that would do, Zach had an inkling when both rushed him, Abner swinging the belt at his face while spearing the dagger at his stomach. The buckle sizzled past Zach's eye as he twisted, parried Abner, twisted again, and parried Will. Never still, he spun to the right.

The fickle throng roared their approval, some clapping as if they were applauding actors in a theater.

"Well done, Injun!"

"Where'd you learn a move like that?"

Zach hadn't learned it anywhere. He was simply reacting, relying on his instincts and his reflexes. His father once told him that the worst mistake a man could make in the heat of combat was to do too much thinking.

"Ten dollars on the Indian!" someone bawled.

Abner was livid, Will gnawing on his lower lip. "On the count of three," Abner called out. "And this time, we don't hold back. We kill him or die trying." Abner resumed swinging the belt. "One!" he yelled.

The crowd fell silent, intent on the outcome.

"Two!" Abner bawled.

Only Zach observed a tall man dressed in an expensive black suit, frilled white shirt, and wide-brimmed black hat step into the open space. His angular features were framed by brown hair graying at the temples. Eyes tinted an icy grayish blue focused on the two rivermen. "That will be enough," he said softly.

Growling like a beast, Abner half-turnerd, his growl fading when he saw the man in black. "You!" he blurted. "What's your stake in this?"

Murmuring broke out, spreading like wildfire. In the front row a stocky man exclaimed, "It's Tyler!"

Will jerked his dagger down as if to hide it behind his leg. "I'm not about to buck you, Mr. Tyler. If you say it's over, it's over. If I'd known this Injun was a friend of yours, I'd never have picked on him."

Abner was fit to be tied. "What the hell are you doing, Will? That 'breed cut me. We're not backing down."

"It's Adam Tyler," Will said.

"So? I can see that for myself," Abner grated. "We don't meddle in his life, he has no right to meddle in ours." He shook his belt at the calm figure in black. "Interfere and we'll bust your skull!"

"You'll try." Adam Tyler had a low, resonant voice that carried far. Holding his right arm out, he bent his elbow and wrist at an odd angle.

Just like that, it was over. The onlookers began to disperse. Abner, grumbling fiercely, trailed Will into the night. Soon only Zach and Adam Tyler were left.

"You possess remarkable skill, young man. My compliments."

Zach was perplexed. Why had a total stranger come to his aid? In light of how the crowd behaved, maybe Tyler was a constable. "They started it. My fiancée and I were minding our own business."

85

"Fiancée? Where is the lady? I'd enjoy meeting her."

Only then did Zach awaken to the terrible truth. He scanned the immediate area and almost shrieked in fury. *Louisa had vanished!*

Chapter Seven

Louisa May Clark's heart was in her throat. She kept pleading for someone to break the fight up, but none of the onlookers were willing. To them it was a spectacle. Great sport. They reveled in the violence. More and more of them shouldered her aside to get a better view, so that within moments she had been pushed from the foremost row to the fourth or fifth.

Lou was intent on the struggle to the exclusion of all else. Although she had every confidence in Zach's prowess, although he could handle himself extremely well, the odds were skewed in favor of his foes. And, too, she fretted that friends of the two rivermen might jump in, which would prove Zach's undoing.

"Oh, please!" she cried. "Won't anyone stop it?"

A recent arrival to the crowd glanced at her. "What's got you so upset, girl? It's just a stinkin' Injun they're fightin'."

Lou contained an urge to kick him where it would hurt the most. She tried to push forward, but a solid wall of broad backs foiled her. "Let me through!" she hollered again and again. For all the effect it had, she might as well be hollering at a real wall of stone and mortar.

That was when a rough hand fell on her shoulder and she was forcibly spun around. Confronting her were three men. Not rivermen or frontiersmen, but city dwellers attired in costly suits and high hats. Two carried mahogany canes. They were all young, all clean-shaven and neatly combed.

"What have we here, gentlemen?" asked the dandy in the center. From under his hat spilled blond curls. The handle of his cane was polished ivory, carved in the shape of a dragon.

"By all that's holy! Ellery, it's a white woman!" replied a companion at his elbow whose brown eyes danced with devilish glee.

"Yet she's dressed like that Indian," chimed in the third.

Ellery raked Lou from head to toe with a look of mild distaste. "This simply won't do, my friends. She's an affront to fashion. I say it's our civic duty to remedy the situation."

Lou resented being manhandled. She resented how they were treating her, how they talked about her as if she weren't even there. Slapping Ellery's manicured hand off her shoulder, she said, "Leave me be!"

"Tart little wench, isn't she?" commented the jackanapes with dancing eyes.

"That she is, Mr. Payne," Ellery said, grinning. "She needs to brush up on her manners as well as her fashion sense."

Payne nudged the third man. "How about you, Bellows? Do you agree? Should we take on the burden of turning this poor wretch into a proper lady?"

Bellows had a smile as oily as his black hair. "All for one and one for all. Isn't that the quaint motto we've adopted, from that new book by that French fellow? Yes, I'm in. If nothing else, this lass will provide us with some small measure of entertainment."

Lou turned, showing her back and her contempt. She saw Zach take a vicious blow. Forgetting about the coxcombs, she attempted to shove past a couple of onlookers, but they refused to budge. "Please!" she pleaded. "For the love of God!"

Once again a hand fell on Lou's shoulder. Seething, she whirled, only to have her wrists seized by Payne and Bellows. Ellery promptly stripped her of all her weapons. "Let go of me!" she objected, seeking to pull from their grasp.

"Not on your life, my dear," Ellery said. "We have appointed you our new mission in life. Or, more appropriately, our mission for the night. So off we go."

The men formed into a wedge, with her in the middle. In a compact knot they pushed outward, away from the circle and the fight. Others were only too eager to let them by, the gap filling immediately with those desiring to witness the outcome.

"No!" Lou shrieked. "You can't! That's my fiancé back there! I can't go anywhere!"

"You're engaged to one of those simpleminded rivermen?" Payne responded. "How crass of you, girl."

Bellows was sharper than he appeared. "By my word, Teddy! I do believe the wench means she's engaged to that other fellow. To the *Indian*."

Ellery glanced at her. "Is that true? You'd stoop so low as to give yourself to a wretched savage?"

"His father is as white as you and I!" Lou declared. She sought to dig in her heels and looked back to see how Zach was faring, but Payne and Bellows jerked her onward. "Damn you! What gives you the right to treat me like this?"

Teddy Payne shook a disapproving finger at her. "A true lady never, ever swears. It's most unbecoming."

"And demeaning," Bellows added. "Why, it's almost as grievous a slight as belching or farting."

The trio laughed. Once more Lou tried to halt, but they hurried on, moving faster as they neared the outskirts of the crowd. They pressed so close against her, she couldn't lift either arm. In desperation she bent to bite Payne's shoulder, but he twisted, then jabbed the tip of his cane into her side.

"None of that, wench! We're doing you a favor. So behave."

"But I don't want you to do me any favors!" Lou said, to no avail. Another few yards brought them to the junction with another street. The dandies slowed, debating which way to go. Their grips slackened.

Lou heaved backward, kicking at the pair holding her. Bellows yelped like a whipped dog. Payne swore and almost lost his hold. But before she could capitalize, Ellery had whirled and grabbed her by the chin.

"Enough! Another such attempt will be soundly punished."

"You can't do this!" Lou reiterated.

Ellery straightened and sniffed. "Obviously, my dear girl, you have no idea who your benefactors are. I am Ellery Quinton Worthington the Third. Teddy, here, is Edward Simon Payne. And that man holding your left arm is none other than Reginald Barclay Bellows."

"Is that supposed to mean something?"

Ellery Quinton Worthington rolled his eyes skyward. "You must be new to St. Louis. Everyone knows who we are. Our families are three of the wealthiest in the city. Our fathers are all high in city government." He said it matter-of-factly. "All we need do is snap our fingers and our every wish is granted. In short, we can do anything we please. So if it amuses us to transform you from a caterpillar into a butterfly, you'll simply have to indulge our whimsy."

"Money is power, my dear," Payne elaborated. "What we want, we get. What we desire to do is as good as done. No one dares oppose us for fear of risking the considerable wrath of our combined families."

90

Bellows puffed out his slim chest. "Why, we once met the President himself, at a banquet my father threw in his honor."

They were moving again, briskly, pedestrians parting like blades of high grass before a strong wind. Ellery strolled along with his cane resting on his shoulder and his high hat tilted at a rakish angle. "St. Louis is *our* city. What we don't own, we influence."

Louisa didn't care how rich and powerful their families were. It didn't give them the right to treat her as their personal plaything. They were spoiled brats, nothing more. She had to bide her time and make a break when a chance presented itself. But waiting was nigh impossible when each step took her farther from Zach. She couldn't shake the gnawing worry that something had happened to him.

The din of the crowd grew fainter with every corner they rounded. Grasping at a straw, Lou said, "If you're truly the gentlemen you pretend to be, you'll let me go this instant."

"Nice try," Ellery said. "But true gentlemen always do what's right. Even when the recipients of their kindness are too dense to appreciate it." Payne and Bellows laughed at his ready wit.

"Why me?" Lou wondered. "Surely you can find someone else to pick on?"

Ellery smiled. "You were convenient, my dear. A perfect remedy to the bane of our existence."

"Boredom," Payne clarified.

Bellows added, "Don't take this personally. Why, just last month we decided to turn a pathetic wretch we found lying in the gutter into a gentleman. It took some doing, I don't mind admitting, but when we took him to our club on a lark, none of the other members guessed the truth."

Payne chuckled. "What great fun that was."

"And now we intend to repeat our triumph," Ellery said.

"We'll treat you to the finest clothes money can buy. We'll take you to the headmistress of a school for young ladies for a few lessons. Before you know it, you'll be a lady yourself."

Lou couldn't believe it. She'd almost rather be in the clutches of Sylvia Banner than these simpletons. "But I don't *want* to be a lady. At least, not the kind you want me to be."

"Your wishes are totally irrelevant," Ellery said. "So hush up."

"Hush," Payne stressed.

"Hush, hush, hush." Bellows wasn't to be outdone.

Lou opened her mouth, but Payne placed a finger to her lips and gave her a stern look. She would love to box each of them on the ears. Better yet, to punch each in the mouth! They weren't truly dangerous, not the way Sylvia had been. Yet their refusal to take no for an answer, their insistence that she go along with their addlepated plans, their use of force to make her comply, were aggravations she could do without.

Another intersection appeared, brightly lit by lamps, filled with people and passing carriages. A knot of nicely dressed women, chatting gaily, drew Lou's attention. Smiling slyly, she marked each step until the women were only yards away, then she suddenly cried out, "Help! Please! These men are abducting me!"

Ellery, Payne, and Bellows all halted, too surprised to say anything. The four women turned toward them.

"They've taken me against my will!" Louisa hollered. "Please do something! I must get back to my fiancé."

A statuesque beauty with raven hair coolly regarded Ellery Quinton Worthington. "Is this true, handsome?"

His reply astounded Lou. "Definitely true, my sweet Venus. We're dragging her off to a horrible fate." Ellery winked. "We're going to introduce this lowly wench to the pleasures of polite society."

The beauty swayed up to him and delicately stroked his chin with a long fingernail painted bright blue. Her eyelids were the same hue, her cheeks dappled with rouge. Perfume reminiscent of lilacs added to her allure. "Then why is she raising such a stink? I'd give anything, Ellery, to have you do the same with me."

Lou was flabbergasted. "You know him?"

"Honey, everyone knows Mr. Worthington and his friends," the beauty answered. "At one time or another all three have paid for my services. And I must say, they are three of the most generous gents anywhere." The other women nodded in agreement.

"Services?" Lou said, then felt her cheeks burn. "Oh. I see. How silly of me."

Ellery was more amused than mad. "We tried to tell you, girl. We know more people than you can imagine. And those we don't know have heard of us. So spare yourself further embarrassment."

The beauty traced the outline of his left ear. "How about me, lover? Is there anything I can do to help?"

"Not that I can think—" Ellery said, then snapped his fingers. "Wait a moment. Perhaps you can, Venus. As I recall, isn't Madame Bovary's shop nearby?"

"Sure is. Care for me to take you there? She's closed at this hour, though."

Ellery patted a pocket on his tailored jacket. "Not to worry. I have just the inducement to convince her to open up."

Venus hooked her elbow with Ellery's and guided them into a side street. Every now and again she would glance over a shapely shoulder at Louisa, plainly curious.

The feeling was mutual. "Is your name really Venus?" Lou inquired.

"Of course not. Most of us in the trade use nicknames. I got mine from a guy who paints and sculpts for a living. Peculiar loon, that one. I always had to tie him to the bedposts and whip him to get him excited. And when we were done, he'd sit and sketch me for hours." Venus laughed. "Men are so strange."

Payne swatted her backside. "And women have room to talk? Remember what you did with that cigar?"

"Only because you asked me to," Venus said.

"No, only because I *paid* you to," Payne amended good-naturedly. "It never ceases to amaze me what money will buy nowadays."

"Cigars are nothing," Venus said. "Remind me to tell you about Phyllis. She has this trick she can do with a flute. You've got to see it to believe it. She can actually—" Venus stopped, her green eyes darting toward Lou. "Well, remind me later."

Ellery twirled his cane. "There's an idea. Maybe we should hold auditions, boys. We'll take a suite at the Imperial. Offer money and clothes as prizes for the most inventive doxies in the city."

"Sheer inspiration," Bellows said. "We'll have categories they can enter in. Music. Dance. Poetry. With more points for those who perform naked."

The dandies and the courtesan cackled, but Louisa didn't share in their mirth. For all their wealth and power, they were unbelievably crude. As for the fallen lovely, Lou had to admit a certain secret fascination. She'd always wondered how any woman with a shred of self-respect would allow a stranger to fondle them. She'd rather slit her throat than live like that.

Payne and Bellows still held her by the wrists, so Lou had no choice but to be steered to a two-story brownstone that billed itself as "Madame Bovary's Palace of Exquisite Finery." A huge window on the bottom floor displayed mannequins dressed in glittering dresses and sparkling jewelry.

"I love to come here to browse and dream," Venus commented.

Payne peered at a mannequin in a bright pink outfit. "Say, I recognize her! She and I frolicked under the sheets once. Talk about wooden lovemaking!"

Bellows roared and clapped him on the back.

"Stiff as could be," Payne quipped.

"Her or you?" Ellery asked as he pounded on the door.

Lou found their humor vulgar. She saw a light come on in an upstairs window. Curtains parted and the sash rose.

"Go away, whoever you are! Can't you see I'm closed?"

Stepping back and craning his neck, Ellery said, "Surely not for me, sweet Bovary! Admit us and you'll make more in one night than you do in a month."

A great moon face poked out. Brown hair fell in ringlets to shoulders gone plump. Lips as thick as sausages flapped. "Who in the world? Worthington, is that you? My old eyes must be deceiving me again. You haven't graced my establishment since last August."

"An oversight I'd like to make up for," Ellery responded. "Throw a robe on and waddle down here, you magnificent hussy."

Madame Bovary's fleshy features creased in mock indignation. "Were anyone else to call me that, I'd drop a vase on their head. But in your case I'll make an exception. You're still the same gloriously vulgar scoundrel you've always been."

"Why tamper with perfection?" was Ellery's rejoinder.

Merry guffaws were cut short by the closing window. Lou glanced at her rifle, which Bellows held, then at her pistol and knife, tucked under Payne's belt. She would give anything to get her hands on a weapon!

Venus had molded herself to Ellery and was puffing lightly on his ear. "After you're done here, lover, how about the two of us go off alone for a while? I've missed you terribly."

"What a marvelous liar you are, vixen," Ellery said. "You've missed my wallet, not me." He nuzzled her neck with relish. "I can't make any promises, my dear. My friends and I are on a crusade."

"We were born in the wrong age," Bellows remarked.

"We should have been knights of the Round Table. Just think! The quest for the Holy Grail. Rescuing damsels in distress. Always chivalrously, of course."

Lou couldn't resist. "What the three of you know about chivalry wouldn't fill a thimble. You're not fit to lick Sir Galahad's feet."

Ellery's smug mask developed a crack. Glowering, he balled a fist as if to strike. "Who are you to judge us, you little witch? You're the one set to marry a damnable heathen."

"I love him!" Lou was itching to kick him where it would hurt most. "He's more of a gentleman, more of a *man*, than you'll ever be."

Quivering with barely contained fury, Ellery took a half-step closer. Suddenly Bellows let go of Lou and gripped his friend by the wrist, preventing him from swinging, and inadvertently sparing him from Lou's foot.

"She's no good to us beaten to a pulp."

"You heard her!" Ellery fumed.

"Obviously, the poor wench has been living on the frontier too long," Bellows said. "She's misguided, is all. She thinks she really cares for that 'breed."

Payne chortled. "We'll set her straight."

Like hell you will! Louisa thought, and vented her seething emotions by kicking Payne in the shin. Yelping like a stricken coyote, he released her. In a twinkling, Lou spun and ran. She had no idea where she was running, no idea which direction she was going. All that mattered was eluding her three abductors and finding Zach.

Shoes pounded in Lou's wake. They were after her. A glance showed Ellery was the fleetest, his contorted features hinting at his intentions if he caught her. But Lou was confident he wouldn't. She was as fit as the proverbial fiddle, her sinews honed by her life in the wilderness. Bounding like an antelope, she gained ground, although not as rapidly as she would have liked. The streets were too crammed, too many people lined the walks. She had to thread through them as if threading through a stand of high-country aspens. Had the streets been deserted, she'd have outdistanced the trio in no time.

Several men with bottles in their hands reared in Lou's path. They were cackling, having a grand old time. She veered to the right to go around, bumping one, who swore lustily and tried to snatch her sleeve. "Sorry!" Lou said, springing past, into the street.

"Land sakes!" one of the others declared. "Was that a girl in those buckskins?"

Lou looked back again to gauge her lead. Belatedly, she registered the hammering of hooves, the clattering of wheels. A speeding carriage was bearing down on her!

"Out of the way!" the driver shouted, making no effort whatsoever to stop.

With hardly a split second to spare, Louisa flung herself to the left. She saved herself from being trampled and run over but not from being clipped by one of the horses. Sent sprawling, she slid onto her hands and knees, scraping them and bruising herself. Frantic, she bolted forward again, all too aware of heavy breathing close behind. The mishap had enabled Ellery to narrow the distance.

"Stop, damn your bones!"

Lou wasn't about to do any such thing. Sprinting madly, avoiding pedestrians, she came to an intersection and bore to the left. By accident she had chosen well. The street was narrower but nowhere near as packed, nor as well lit. Even better, it led into a residential area, with hedges and trees and broad yards.

"Don't make this harder than it has to be!" Ellery called out.

Lou smiled to herself. He could threaten all he wanted. She was in her element now. Giving them the slip would be child's play for someone who had eluded Piegans and

Utes. Slanting toward a gap in a high hedge, she sped into the opening and on across a neatly trimmed yard dotted by towering maples. At the next one she came to, Lou stopped to check on her pursuers.

Ellery and Payne were just inside the hedge, Payne doubled over and wheezing. Neither was in the best of shape. Lack of exercise had sapped their stamina, had rendered them soft, whereas Lou's life in the mountains had made her as tough as whipcord.

"They'll never catch me now," Lou softly vowed. Keeping the trunk between them, she ran toward a huge mansion. Gleaming marble columns and a magnificent portico testified to the wealth of its owners. She realized she was in a wealthy section of the city, maybe the very section where her three tormentors lived. How fitting, she thought, to lose them there.

No lights showed in any of the windows. The owners were either asleep or gone. Lou swung wide of the porch, thankful for deep shadow that cloaked her like an inky glove, and jogged toward the rear. She made no more noise than the breeze.

Presently a new obstacle presented itself. To Lou's consternation, she was confronted by a wall seven feet high. She relaxed when she saw it was covered with ivy. Climbing over would pose no problem.

Lou had only twenty feet to cover when something growled, to the right. She looked, her blood chilling at the sight of a powerfully built black dog that had materialized out of the darkness, its lips pulled back over gleaming fangs. Lou hoped against hope it was tied or chained, but the next moment it barked ferociously and charged.

The dog was twice as far from Lou as she was from the wall, but it was moving twice as fast. She fairly flew, her heart racing, the slavering canine streaking toward her like a Sioux arrow.

Lou wouldn't make it. Not if she ran up to the wall and tried to scale it. So she did the only other thing she could. When she was seven or eight feet away, she girded herself and vaulted upward, leaping for all she was worth, her fingers hooked to catch hold of the dangling ivy.

Teeth gnashed at Lou's heels. She felt brief, lancing pain where the dog nipped her. Then she was hurtling through the air. She hit harder than she anticipated, nearly knocking the breath from her lungs. The ivy wasn't as thick or as strong as it had appeared. Lou grabbed for purchase, but the slim strands wouldn't hold. Scrabbling wildly, she sought to cling on.

Below her was the black dog, froth rimming its mouth. Barking and snarling, it coiled, then arced at her legs.

Fear enabled Lou to cling on, and she heaved higher as shearing teeth snapped shut inches from her calves. Her upthrust arm hooked the top of the wall, and for a moment she hung there, as weak as a newborn kitten. But the weakness didn't last. Again the dog sprang, galvanizing Lou into pulling herself onto the top of the wall, where she lay for a bit catching her breath while the frustrated animal jumped and snarled and howled.

Lou glanced toward the front of the mansion. Ellery and Payne would come on the run and blunder smack into the dog. She chuckled. It couldn't happen to two more deserving people. Carefully lowering herself over the other side, Lou dropped lightly to the ground. She was in another narrow street, even more dimly lit. Lou turned to the left. If memory served, that was the direction which would eventually take her back to the bawdy house—and her darling Zachary. She was in dire fear for his life, afraid the rivermen had slain him.

The wall ended at an intersection. Lou stepped into the open and paused to listen for the racket sure to break out when the dog spied Ellery and Payne. Instead, she heard the metallic rasp of the hammer of her own Hawken being thumbed back and felt the jab of the muzzle against her arm.

"Don't so much as twitch," Reginald Barclay Bellows said. "As a general rule, I don't believe in harming the fairer sex, but in your case, you little savage, I'll happily make an exception."

Chapter Eight

Zachary King was beside himself with anxiety. He dashed from one side of the street to the other, seeking the woman he loved. The awful truth brought him to a stunned stop, and he blurted, "She's gone! She's really gone!"

"No one ever disappears into thin air," said the man who had broken up the fight. "We'll find her, son."

Zach was mad enough to battle a grizzly barehanded. "I'm not your son!" he declared. Zach didn't know why Adam Tyler had come to his aid, and he really didn't care. Other than old George Milhouse, he hadn't met one white in St. Louis he'd trust farther than he could throw a buffalo.

"A figure of speech," the man in black said. "I meant no insult." He smoothed his sleeve. "I've never had a son of my own, so I reckon I've taken to calling most everyone younger than me that, out of habit."

Zach turned. Tyler's expression was kindly, but bitter experience had taught Zach that sometimes a man's right hand was offered in seeming friendship while the left clutched a hidden knife. "Why did you butt in?" he demanded.

Adam Tyler shrugged. "It wasn't a fair fight, for one thing. For another, I've never been fond of rivermen. They're poor losers."

"Poor losers?"

"I gamble for a living. And more often than not, when I beat rivermen at cards, they groan and moan and mutter threats. Not to my face, you understand."

"They were scared of you," Zach recalled.

"To be exact, it's my reputation they fear. I've been in a few duels over the years. Barroom gossip has embellished the stories to where everyone thinks I'm one of the deadliest gents on the Mississippi. Or anywhere else," Tyler added offhandedly.

"My pa saw a duel once," Zach mentioned. "Almost twenty years ago, when he was on his way west." His father had related the tale many times, at Zach's enthralled request. "In Illinois, at an inn where he was lodging overnight. Two gamblers—"

Tyler tensed. "Illinois? Two decades ago? Was the inn called the Cork and Crown, by any chance?"

"Why, yes, it was," Zach confirmed in astonishment. "How did you know?"

The gambler shared Zach's amazement. "I'll be damned. This world of ours is smaller than we imagine. That was your father I befriended? I never learned anything about him—who he was or where he came from." Tyler shook his head. "I can't believe it's been that long. All of a sudden I feel as ancient as Methuselah." He touched his side, low down. "I was one of those gamblers. The other was a blowhard by the name of Noah Clancy. He cheated during the duel and shot me in the back, but I blew out his wick."

"You live in St. Louis now?"

Tyler nodded. "I have for years, plying my trade on various riverboats and at the best gambling dens in the city.

Your guardian angel must be watching over you, to bring us together like this. If anyone can help you find your fiancée, I can."

"How?" Zach asked. The crowd had dispersed, everyone going on about their business except for a few stragglers who were more interested in the man in black than in him. Tyler walked toward a bench occupied by a skinny, wizened bundle of bones in a tattered coat and baggy, torn pants, who was sipping from a silver flask.

"Donovan," the gambler said.

The man jerked the flask down as if it had scorched his lips. Squinting out of bloodshot eyes, he said, "Oh, Adam! It's you, old friend! Haven't jawed with you in a quite a spell. How have you been?"

"Can't complain," Tyler said. "And you?"

"Hard at work drinkin' myself into oblivion," Donovan answered. "Another year or so and I reckon I'll succeed. Then I can join my sweet Marcy and baby Jessica in the hereafter." He took an overly long swig and smacked his lips. "Might even be sooner, the Lord willin'."

The gambler pulled a wad of bills from an inner jacket pocket and peeled several off. "Perhaps this will help. In return for a little information, if you'd be so kind."

"Anything," Donovan said cheerfully.

"You witnessed the dispute a short while ago involving this young man?" Tyler asked.

The drunkard peered intently at Zach. "That I did. It was a good scrape." He took another swig. "What's your name, youngster?"

Chafing at the delay, Zach introduced himself.

"His fiancée was with him," Tyler elaborated. "I suspect you saw what became of her, and we'd very much like to know."

"That gal in buckskins?" Donovan sniffed the air and scrunched up his nose as if at a foul stench. "It was those three cocky brats. The lords of St. Louis, they style themselves. But between you and me, the three of them com-

103

bined ain't worth a soggy pile of dog droppin's. I still remember that time they were beatin' on me with their damanable canes and you came along."

Tyler, Zach saw, had grown as flinty as a Blackfoot on the warpath. "Ellery and his bootlickers took her? Did you happen to overhear where they were headed?"

Donovan treated himself to more whiskey. "Nope. Sorry. There's never any tellin' with that bunch." Capping the flask, he unbuttoned his shirt and slid it underneath for safekeeping. "Sittin' over here by my lonesome, I couldn't help but notice, though. She didn't look none too pleased."

Zach was anxious to begin the hunt. "You know these men?" he asked the gambler. "Then what are we waiting for?" Whoever they were, they would suffer. Zach had gone easy on Sylvia Banner and Titus, but he wouldn't make the same mistake again.

"We can't go off half-cocked," Tyler said. "St. Louis covers a lot of area. It would take weeks to find her blundering around like waifs in a snowstorm."

"What would they want with her, anyway?" Zach asked.

Donovan was folding the money. "Now, there's a hare-brained question, boy. Those three will bed any female they take a shine to, whether the female is inclined or not."

Smoldering like fireplace coals, Zach would have marched off then and there if not for a hail from the steps of the Gilded Lily. Down them hustled George Milhouse, pumping his hickory walking stick. Showing more teeth than a politician on the stump, he hurried over, saying, "I found out where Festerman lives! By dawn this will all be over and we can get on with our lives." Milhouse scanned the street. "Say, who are these fellers? And where the devil is Louisa?"

Adam Tyler had questions of his own. "Festerman? Lon Festerman? The single most dangerous man in the city? Exactly what are you involved in, Zachary King?"

More precious minutes were wasted while Zach explained. The old trapper and the gambler hit it off, but

Zach was too impatient to twiddle his thumbs while they became better acquainted. "I'm going after Lou," he announced, hefting the Hawken. "Festerman will keep until she's safe."

"Go ahead," Tyler said. "Waste the whole night searching. Waste tomorrow, too, and the next day. If she's still alive when you finally track her down, tell her it took you so long because you wouldn't listen to reason."

"Talk, talk, talk," Zach said. "White men are like chipmunks!"

"But we're smart chipmunks," Tyler said. "Ever hear of anyone catching fish in a desert? Or hunting elk in a swamp?"

Zach didn't see what that had to do with anything, and said so.

"I'm not much of a hunter, but I know a man hunts game where it's most likely to be found. And I might know where to find Ellery Quinton Worthington the Third and his friends. I travel in some of the same social circles. Or, rather, gaming circles."

Milhouse poked Zach with the walking stick. "I'd listen to him, boy. You'll find your filly a lot quicker."

Zach had never been fond of having to depend on others, but he would make an exception in this instance. "Where do we go first?"

"My place," Adam Tyler said.

Donovan piped up. "What about me? I can't shoot straight anymore, but I can be of help if you'll let me."

"Not this time." The gambler placed a hand on the other's stooped shoulder. "Ellery and his crowd aren't above slitting throats when it suits them. It's safer if you're well out of it."

"I ain't scared," Donovan said.

Zach believed him. The drunk was courting death, not shunning it. Zach inquired why as Tyler led Milhouse and him to the south.

"About a year ago, Donovan's wife and baby girl were

105

wiped out in a smallpox epidemic," the man in black revealed. "Oh, I know what you're thinking. That can happen to anyone. But Donovan had sent them to his uncle's farm at the first sign of the outbreak so they would be safe. Only thing is, hardly anyone in St. Louis came down with it. The epidemic struck hardest out in the country. His wife and daughter were among the first to die."

Milhouse's walking stick was tapping the ground in regular cadence. "They'd have lived if he hadn't sent them away. Is that what he believes?"

"Wouldn't you? Which is the reason he's been slowly drinking himself into an early grave." Tyler frowned up at the stars. "Anyone who claims life is fair must walk around with blinders on."

"There's nothing worse than losing a loved one," Milhouse said. "It tears a body up inside. They're never the same."

"Truer words were never spoken," Tyler agreed.

Zach was thinking of Louisa, thinking of how torn up he would be if anything happened to her. He shuddered at the prospect. The only consolation would be his own end. Not a slow and agonizing one, like Donovan's. His would be swift and bloody, just as his vengeance on those who dared harm her would be. He caught the man in black studying him. "What's on your mind?"

"I was just wondering what size pants you wear."

Zachary King thrust out his jaw like a riled bull and flatly declared, "I refuse. I won't do it, and that's that."

"Do you want to save your fiancée?" Adam Tyler retorted, holding out clothes he had selected from a chest of drawers and a closet. "Take these and try them on. You're big for your age, so they might fit. If they do, they're yours to keep."

"My own are just fine, thank you." Zach was grateful for the offer, but he couldn't quite bring himself to accept.

George Milhouse stirred in his chair. "You acting like a ten-year-old. We can't waltz into any of Festerman's places with you wearing Shoshone buckskins. You saw for your-self what happened at the Gilded Lily."

As if he were handling a live skunk, Zach reluctantly accepted the clothes but held them at arm's length. "I've never worn any quite like these before."

"They go on one sleeve at a time, like most." Tyler gestured at a doorway. "Change in the bedroom. Give a yell if you need help."

"Help getting dressed?" Zach laughed. That would be the day. He did as they requested, closing the door to ensure privacy. Removing his buckskins was like removing his own skin, and he stood for a few moments, stark naked, debating whether to put them back on. He had to remind himself that Milhouse and Tyler had his best interests at heart. They were as keen on finding Lou as he was. So he decided to go along with their wishes.

Zach's father owned a suit, but Zach had seldom seen Nate wear it. There was that time a missionary visited their cabin, and that social the trappers put on for a pair of schoolteachers bound for the Oregon country. Usually, though, the suit gathered dust. And now that Zach had an opportunity to try one on for himself, he understood the reason.

The gambler's gift included striped trousers, a double-breasted navy blue frock coat, a a striped tartan vest, and a white shirt. Zach had no problem donning them, but the trousers were uncomfortably tight and itched, the white shirt had a stiff collar that chafed his skin whenever he twisted his neck, and the vest had the same pattern as the kilts he had seen Scotsmen wear at the annual rendezvous and which he'd always thought were so ridiculous. Not that he ever said so to any of the Scotsmen. Once a drunk trapper had made a few unkind remarks about men who wore dresses and been treated to a beating Zach never forgot.

Now Zach picked up a long silken tie—cravats, he believed they were called—and was completely stumped. Try as he might, he couldn't tie it right. And he couldn't see how anyone else could, either. It was harder than braid-ing hair.

Tyler and Milhouse were sipping brandy and chatting when Zach emerged. The old trapper, about to swallow, sputtered like a foundering whale, brandy shooting out his nostrils.

The gambler, as always, was more reserved. Grinning, he raised his long-stemmed glass in salute. "My compli-ments, young sir. Once we tuck your hair down the back of your jacket, no one will look at you twice."

"What about this?" Zach showed them the crumpled cravat.

"Don't let it vex you. I was sixteen before I learned how to tie one." Tyler rose. "Secretly, I've long harbored the idea they were invented by a lunatic to drive the rest of us crazy." His grin widened. "Cravats and corsets are the bane of a gentleman's existence."

Milhouse roared, although why, Zach couldn't guess. He stood stiffly while the gambler affixed the cravat and then stepped back to appraise him.

"Half the men in St. Louis would give their pokes to look half as good as you do, son" was the man in black's assessment.

Zach didn't mind being called "son" this time, but being praised for his appearance made him vaguely uncomfort-able. The truth be known, he had never given his looks much thought. Fussing over it always struck him as downright vain. A person was born the way they were. That was that.

"It will also help if you puff yourself up and act as if you have a lot of money," George Milhouse suggested. "Then no one will care whether you're a 'breed."

Being reminded of the incident at the Gilded Lily aroused Zach's anger. "I'm ready. What are we waiting for?"

"One final touch," Tyler said. Going to a cabinet, he opened the glass door and removed an elaborate polished box, which he set on a table. Nestled on red velvet inside were a pair of exquisite pistols, a matched set of dueling flintlocks that cost more than all the guns in the King family combined. Tyler loaded one, then the other, reversed his grip on each, and offered them to Zach.

"I have my own, plus my rifle."

"You can't take that cannon of yours into the sort of establishments Ellery and his friends frequent." Tyler pushed the pistols into Zach's hands. "Trust me. Use these. They fire true. And when in Rome, remember?"

"This is St. Louis," Zach said, confused.

"Never mind."

The two grown men swapped chuckles. Zach shoved the flintlocks under his belt and stalked to the door. "*Now* can we go?"

Tyler's light mood evaporated like dew under a blazing sun. "Yes, indeed. We're off to rescue the fair damsel in distress."

"And to core the brains of any sons of bitches who get in our road," the old trapper added, standing.

"You're staying here," Tyler said.

"Like hell I am."

"I don't have clothes that will fit you," the gambler said.

"So? I got into the Gilded Lily, didn't I?"

"Only because you're white. Where I'm taking young Zach, even that isn't enough." Tyler fished a bottle from a cupboard. "Make yourself to home. God willing, we'll be back with the lady by morning."

Zach was surprised when the feisty oldster sank back into the chair without further protest.

"Be that way. Just don't blame me if your damn bottle is empty."

Their first stop was at the Golden Bough. Zach had never seen so much brass and glass and gold gilt in all his born days. The doorman greeted them with a warm smile, ushering them indoors with a grand gesture.

"Mr. Tyler, sir! It's been a while since you favored us with a visit."

"Then I'm overdue, aren't I?" Tyler suavely responded, flicking a bill that the doorman slid as neatly as could be under his coat.

"Always a treat to have you here, sir."

The other employees of the gambling den were equally courteous. They welcomed the tall man in black as if he were visiting royalty, bending over backwards in their zeal to please him. Even other patrons, Zach noted, took special interest in Adam Tyler, pointing and whispering as he passed by.

"I had no idea you were so famous," Zach said.

"Not fame, my friend. Notoriety."

"There's a difference?"

"Fame endures. George Washington will rightly be famous as long as our great country exists." Tyler bestowed a smile on a charming female admirer. "Notoriety, on the other hand, is the fashion of the moment. It's a two-edged sword. If circumstances work out right, as in the case of Jim Bowie, notoriety can result in lasting fame. But more often than not it leads to an early grave and paid mourners."

Zach wasn't sure he fully understood. But one thing he did know. Call it fame, call it notoriety, there were worse things than having beautiful women fawn over a man and others wait on him hand and foot.

The Golden Bough catered to the city's wealthiest, to those who could afford to lose incredible sums of money and not bat an eye. Plush wine-red carpet cushioned every step. Gilded mirrors adorned the walls, and massive chandeliers glittered overhead. The dealers, floormen, bartenders were dressed in outfits that matched the color of the carpet.

Zach was just as dazzled by the exclusive clientele. Elegant women in shimmering gowns wore sparkling jewelry worth a fortune. Men in silk high hats and long coats sported gold fob watches, rings, and cravat pins, their hands as neatly manicured as those of the women, their mustaches waxed, their every hair perfect.

Scores of tables accommodated diverse gambling tastes. There were card games of every kind. There was roulette and dice and faro. Wreathed in cigar and cigarette smoke, players lost extravagant sums with a nonchalance that was as calculated a sham as their haughty airs.

Here and there, though, were men who were different, men cut from a different cloth, men who, like Adam Tyler, stood out from the rest by virtue of their bearing and their somber attire. They were wolves among sheep, professional gamblers, those who made a living at the trade, not merely dabbled in it for sport or amusement.

Tyler made for the back of the main room. Zach was close behind. Many gave him inquisitive stares, but no one had the audacity to challenge him. Maybe it was Tyler's presence. Or maybe, Zach mused, it was just as Tyler had said: In his new clothes he fit right in.

A door ahead was flanked by a pair of brawny men in wine-red jackets. The older of the two dipped his chin in respect as the tall gambler approached.

"Mr. Tyler! Have you come to grace us with your play, sir? Your last game is still a frequent topic of discussion."

"I'm here to see LeBeau," the man in black answered. "I trust he's here tonight?"

"And almost every night. Some might say it is his home away from home."

Tyler smiled and strode through the gilded doorway. Then he did a strange thing, in Zach's estimation. Tyler quickly stepped to the right, putting his back to the wall, and held his right arm at the same odd angle he had held it when confronted by the pair of rowdy rivermen in front of the Gilded Lily.

Zach's eyebrows arched in a silent question.

"Enemies, son," Tyler said so only Zach heard. "I have many. I must always be vigilant."

At a large circular table covered in wine-red cloth sat five men dressed in the absolute best apparel riches could purchase. Four were of little interest to Zach, but the fifth

111

man merited more than a random gaze. He was big, a human moon, so round in the center it was a wonder he could move his short arms across his chest and stomach. Twinkling blue eyes regarded the world at large with intelligence and humor, and they twinkled brighter when the man in black neared the table.

"*Sacre mere!* Can it be? Do my senses deceive me?"

"Hello, LeBeau," Tyler said.

"Adam! *Mon ami! Ou avez-vous ete?*"

"I've been around."

LeBeau beckoned. "Come here and give me a hug, you delightful bandit. To deprive us of your company for so long is a crime!"

Zach thought the overstuffed Frenchman was a simpleton, but Adam Tyler seemed to place great stock in him. Tyler walked over and let LeBeau pull him down for a peck on both cheeks. The other players had lowered their cards and did not act at all disturbed by the intrusion.

"To what do we owe this honor, Tyler?" asked a stiff-backed gentleman with gray temples. "Do you want to sit in?"

"Not tonight, Carson." The man in black adjusted his right sleeve. "Ellery Quinton Worthington the Third. He and his two friends, Bellows and Payne."

LeBeau was reaching for a glass of port. His pudgy fingers froze in midair and he glanced up sharply. "What about them, *mon ami?*"

"I'm looking for them."

An electric ripple charged the room. LeBeau and Carson exchanged glances. Then the Frenchman said much too casually, "You jest, *non?* They deserve it, I grant you. But their fathers would make formidable enemies."

Tyler pulled out a chair, reversed it, and sat with his arm draped across the chair back. "What's one more, more or less, eh?"

LeBeau leaned toward his friend. Where the Frenchman's belly pressed against the table, Zach saw no telltale folds of fat or flab. It dawned on him that LeBeau's bulk was mainly muscle, and that the Frenchman might be a formidable adversary in his own right.

"I beg you to think this out, *mon ami*. Many times I have wanted to squash them like the bugs they are. But their families would put such a price on my head it would not be worth the fleeting pleasure."

Adam Tyler said nothing.

"He's right, you know," Carson said. "In our profession we must choose our enemies carefully. Weigh the odds. And if the cost is more than the affront, let it go."

"I can't," Tyler said.

"Why the hell not?" Carson asked. "What could they possibly have done? Insulted your honor? Even Ellery wouldn't be that stupid."

Everyone grinned except Tyler.

LeBeau shifted his attention to Zach, his forehead knitting. "What have we here? Have you brought us new blood, Adam?" LeBeau tapped his pudgy chin with his pudgy fingertips. "This young gentleman wouldn't have anything to do with your newfound death wish, would he?"

Tyler's continued silence bothered Zach. It was only making the others more curious. "Mr. Tyler has offered to help me," he said.

LeBeau and Carson both nodded knowingly. "I thought as much," the Frenchman declared. "I am Henri LeBeau, by the way, at your service, monsieur. Any friend of Adam's is a friend of mine, *non*?" LeBeau coughed. "And in what capacity, might I inquire, has our mutual friend offered his help?"

Zach looked at Tyler to see if the man in black would mind if he explained, but Adam Tyler's expression was impossible to read. "We believe Worthington and his friends have taken my fiancée."

"Taken her?" LeBeau said. "You mean, they have had their way with her?"

The skin under Zach's stiff collar grew hot. "They'd better not have," he said, his throat constricted with emotion. "She's never even been with—" Zach stopped. In his turmoil he had said more than he should have.

LeBeau's saucer eyes widened. "A virgin? In St. Louis? Can such a miracle really be?"

Zach was becoming hotter. "We're just in from the mountains—"

"So! Now all is clear." LeBeau sighed and stared at Tyler. "Lost puppies and kittens again, *non*? When will you learn, *mon ami*? I do not deny the purity, but I question your judgment." He paused, and when the man in black still wouldn't comment, LeBeau looked right at Zach and said, "He's digging his grave with this one."

Chapter Nine

"What do you think, dearie?" Madame Bovary asked.

Louisa May Clark gazed at her reflection in the full-length mirror and fumed. They didn't want to hear what she really thought, not as mad as she was. The three dandies had dragged her back to the Palace of Exquisite Finery and were now standing guard downstairs to prevent her from escaping a second time. Madame Bovary, bundled in a tent of a robe, with the willing help of winsome Venus, had been given the task of transforming Lou "from a caterpillar into a butterfly," in Ellery's words, or from a "dull duck into a radiant swan," as Payne put it.

"You look lovely," Venus complimented her. "I wish I could afford clothes as fine and pretty as those."

Lou didn't feel fine. She didn't feel pretty. She felt abused, used, treated like the personal plaything of her abductors. The dress she now wore did little to soothe her. She'd as soon rip it off as shoot the whole bunch of them.

"Sure took some doing, didn't it?" Madame Bovary

said. "Now, you know why I kept my robe on. Getting dressed can take forever."

Lou gave a very unladylike snort. That had to be the understatement of the century. They had spent over two hours dressing her. Two hours! With Madame Bovary's sweaty hands always pawing, poking, prodding. And with Venus clumsily trying to help but putting her hands where they would create the most confusion. The two older women had to do all the work because Lou refused to lift a finger. She balked at doing anything that Ellery, Payne, and Bellows wanted.

Madame Bovary didn't have that luxury. Ellery had made it plain that unless he was immensely pleased with the results, there would be hell to pay. His exact words were. "You'll find that rumors are spreading to the effect your clothes are outdated and overpriced, and no one with any sense would ever shop here."

Bovary wasn't intimidated. She set to work in earnest. First the women wrestled Lou out of her buckskins. Literally. Lou vigorously resisted until Madame Bovary sat on her. The two women then pried them off, and Madame Bovary, sniffing in disdain, tossed them into a corner.

"How revolting! What possessed you to wear animal hides when there are so many refined garments available?"

Lou didn't inform them she was fresh in from the wilds, or that in the mountains buckskins were preferred by most Indians and whites alike. Buckskin was durable. It resisted water, it insulated against cold and heat. Store-bought garments wouldn't last a week in the wilderness.

Next, Madame Bovary measured Lou from neck to ankles, then waddled downstairs. On her return she brought an armful of clothes, which she set in a chair.

Lou had to submit to the indignity of a knee-length chemise and stockings held up by garters. Droopy drawers completed her underwear.

From the pile Madame Bovary took a corset and held it to Lou's waist. "You need this, dearie, about as much as I need to gain ten pounds. What do you eat? Birdseed? You're as thin as a rail."

Lou was spared the corset, but not from having to wear four petticoats. Each in itself was heavy and felt cumbersome, but four weighed her down like an anchor. Every step was like wading through cold porridge.

"It's not that bad," Madame Bovary said when Lou complained. "Haven't you ever worn petticoats before?"

Lou was too embarrassed to confess she hadn't. Her mother wore plain ones, not the elaborately trimmed affairs Madame Bovary specialized in, made from pure white cotton and embroidered with lace and colored trim.

The dress came last, and finding the right one gave Madame Bovary no end of headaches. She tried on one after another, but none pleased her. One was too drab, another was too brown, another was proportioned all wrong, one bunched up at the bottom.

Eventually, perfection was achieved. Madame Bovary settled on a silk two-piece peach dress with elbow-length sleeves, black silk fringe, and black velvet trim. The lacy bodice was trimmed with small gold-gilt buttons. It had a narrow waist and flared wide at the hem, covering the new stiff shoes forced onto Lou's feet.

"What do you think, dearie?" Madame Bovary repeated herself.

"The moment those bastards turn their backs, I'm ripping this monstrosity off," Lou pledged.

"Lord in heaven, don't!" Bovary said. "It will cost Ellery three hundred and sixty-two dollars."

"All the more reason to rip it," Lou argued.

"What do you have against being beautiful?" Madame Bovary asked. "Every woman has a duty to look the best she possibly can at all times. It's why I opened my shop."

Venus was admiring her own reflection. "That, and the money."

Madame Bovary tugged on one of Lou's sleeves. "I'll have you know my apparel is worth every penny. I import

117

only the very best, or have dresses made for me by the most skilled seamstresses in the city. You're just jealous because you don't have a shop of your own."

"I will one day," Venus said. "Once I've saved up enough."

Bovary glanced at the raven-haired lovely, the pink tip of her tongue poking between her thick lips. "You're serious? Why don't you stop by tomorrow evening after I close the shop. I can give you the benefit of my experience."

"I'd like that," Venus said, and giggled girlishly.

They had momentarily forgotten about Lou, and she sidled toward the door, but she had taken only four steps when a ponderous hand closed on her arm and jerked her back in front of the mirror.

"Where do you think you're sneaking off to?" Madame Bovary demanded. "We're not done yet."

"What's left?" Lou asked.

"Your hair, for starters. Then your nails. And correct me if I'm wrong, but you're not wearing a streak of makeup, are you?"

Venus was horrified. "She isn't?"

"There ought to be a law," Madame Bovary said, shaking her head. "Are you too lazy to dab on a little rouge in the morning? Or apply some color to line your eyes?"

Lou simmered like a boiling teapot. "My fiancé likes me just how I am, I'll have you know."

"Then he's as big an idiot as you are." Madame Bovary wasn't one to mince words. "As my dear great-grandmother always reminded us Bovary girls, beauty is as beauty does. In other words, you can be the ugliest gosling this side of purgatory, but if you wear nice clothes and do up your hair and face, you'll come across as positively gorgeous."

"Beauty doesn't kill grizzly bears," Lou said.

The folds of Madame Bovary's throat bobbed. "Were you hit on the head by an anvil when you were little? What does that have to do with anything?"

"In the Rockies it isn't how pretty a woman is that counts," Lou said. "It's how fast and accurate she can shoot, how well she can hunt and track, how good she is at skinning and cooking game."

Bovary's body quivered like a bowl of pudding. "I couldn't conceive of a more wretched existence. Women aren't men. We shouldn't go around doing the things they do." She pointed at Lou's buckskins. "And we certainly shouldn't dress like them."

"A woman can hunt and fish and whatnot and still be all female," Lou said.

"A woman, maybe, but not a *lady*. A lady's only concern is how well she's dressed, whether her hair is coiffed and her nails painted and her lips as red as they can be." Madame Bovary fluffed at Lou's bangs. "I'm living proof my great-grandmother knew what she was talking about."

Lou couldn't help herself. "You are?"

"Take a good look at me, dearie. I'm old and I'm fat, but no one has ever called me ugly. Do you know why? Because I dress in the best clothes money can buy. I always look beautiful, even if I'm not. So everyone comes to me for beauty advice. Me! Ethel Winklemeyer, who grew up on a farm and wore burlap dresses and straw hats the first twelve years of her life."

"You changed your name to Madame Bovary?"

"It's all part of the illusion, child. If there's one lesson I've learned, it's that people will pick illusion over reality any day of the week."

Venus was stupefied by the revelation. "You were raised on a farm? With cows and chickens and sheep?"

Madame Bovary laughed. "Honey, I'm an old hog slopper from who flung the chunk. But I'm not about to let any of my clientele know."

"You've told me," Venus said.

"And if you ever tell anyone, I'll have your scrawny neck broken and your carcass tossed in the river." Madame

David Thompson

Bovary said it sweetly, playfully, yet without the warmth and smile that marked real humor.

"Why are you telling us this?" Lou asked.

"Because in half an hour you'll be going downstairs, and if you don't pass muster, Ellery will not only punish you, he'll punish me, as well." Bovary pulled her green robe tighter around her ample bosom. "I can do without his aggravation, thank you very much. Which is why I want you to sashay on down there as if you're the Queen of Egypt. Hold your head high and swing your hips, and Ellery and his boys will rate you the loveliest lady who ever drew breath."

"But I'm not," Lou argued. "I'm a beanpole. A tomboy, my pa always called me."

"Weren't you listening to a word I just said?" Madame Bovary upbraided her. "You know that you're a hayseed and I know that you're a hayseed, but that doesn't mean you have to *act* like a hayseed. Act like a lady and snooty Ellery Quinton Worthington the Third won't know the damn difference."

Walking down the stairs was one of the hardest things Lou ever did. Not because she hated the three dandies and naturally resented doing what they wanted. Not because she was worried sick about Zach and couldn't think straight. Nor because Madame Bovary and Venus were poised to push her if she balked.

No, it was because deep down in the wellspring of her being, where Lou's innermost thoughts and desires thrived, a tiny part of her *wanted* to be beautiful. For the first and only time in her life, to actually be *pretty*.

When she was little, Lou had always been a gangly girl who would rather play with the boys than her own gender. She had held her own in footraces, at wrestling, at flinging rocks, and the hundred and one other pastimes boys enjoyed. At school she'd always worn homespun britches crafted by her mother. While they were always clean and neat, no one could accuse her mother of having much of a flair for fashion.

Lou had been the plainest of the plain. To her family and friends she'd always joked about her lack of elegance and claimed it didn't upset her. But she was fibbing, for in her heart of hearts she craved to be beautiful. To be the sort of woman who turned heads. Who made all activity around her stop.

Oh, Lou had seen it happen. She had seen women who were so stunning it defied belief, as if God deliberately lavished more beauty on some than others. Jessica Parker, a childhood acquaintance, had been one of the blessed. Jessica had been the envy of every girl and the desire of every boy. Later in life, Jessica married the banker's son, the most eligible bachelor in four counties.

Many a time, Lou had watched Jessica stroll down the street, golden hair aglow, an angel in earthly apparel, surrounded by girls who just wanted to be seen in her company and trailed by a passel of lovestruck boys.

"Pathetic," Lou had always said. Yet deep down she wasn't fooling anyone, least of all herself. There wasn't a girl alive who wouldn't give everything they owned, and maybe their soul in the bargain, if they could be as attractive as Jessica Parker.

So now, as Lou slowly descended the steps, she found herself doing as Madame Bovary had advised. Lou held her head high, her chin out. She walked as Jessica Parker had always done, all too conscious of the rouge and the other makeup. Lou's mother would roll over in her grave if she could see the change that had taken place.

Ellery, Payne, and Bellows were waiting in the dress shop proper. Lou heard them and slowed, losing her nerve.

". . . much longer?" Edward Payne was asking. "They've been at it long enough to turn a warthog into a thoroughbred."

"We'll give them another half an hour," Ellery said.

"Then let's have some real fun," Reginald Bellows proposed. "Drinking, gambling, wenching."

Payne made a sound like a constipated goat. "We do that every night. I was hoping our little savage would provide us with some diversion, but so far she's been more of a pain than a pleasure."

The stairwell was in shadow. None of them spotted Lou until she was at the bottom, her hand on the brass rail, her pose as unlike her normal posture as the dress she wore was unlike her buckskins.

Payne was lifting the hem of a garment on a mannequin to peek up at the mannequin's legs when he happened to spy Lou's reflection in the front window. Spinning, he let out a long breath and exclaimed, "Pinch me and prove I'm not dreaming!"

Bellows turned and whistled.

That left Ellery, who rotated slowly and then blinked as if he'd been poked in the eyes. "Bovary is a wizard!" Excitedly waving his cane, he came over and examined Louisa from the crown of her head to the soles of her feet, sniffing loudly all the while. "I'll be damned. If it looks like a lady and smells like a lady and—" Ellery ran a hand over Lou's shoulder, over the smooth silk. "—feels like a lady, then it must be the genuine article."

"We've outdone ourselves!" Payne declared merrily.

"Hear, hear!" Bellows seconded the motion. "We could take her to any of our usual haunts and she wouldn't raise an eyebrow."

Ellery leaned close again to sniff the perfume Bovary had dabbed on Lou's hair and neck. "That remains to be seen, and is, after all, the point of this whole exercise. I vote we escort Miss Clark to one of them and put it to the test. Or, rather, put *her* to the test."

"Not so fast." Madame Bovary was leaning against the rail, her left palm outstretched. "You promised to make it worth my while, Mr. Worthington. And the entire city knows you're a man of your word."

"Flatterer," Ellery said. From an inner pocket he drew a leather poke, which he jiggled. Coins jangled, and opening the drawstring, Ellery plucked one out and held it to the lamp. It was solid gold, and as big around as a walnut.

"How's this for a start?" He flipped it straight up, end over end.

Madame Bovary could move surprisingly quick when she wanted. Her hand snaked out and caught the coin as slickly as a juggler would catch a falling apple. "An eagle? Ten dollars wouldn't even begin to cover the cost of the rouge I used."

"There are twenty more in my poke," Ellery said, and tossed it to her.

"That's still nowhere near enough, handsome."

Ellery looked at Lou, his mouth pinched. "Silk and lace adds up, doesn't it? But since you've far surpassed our expectations, my dear, I have no regrets." Flourishing a wad of bills thick enough to gag a horse, he began filling Bovary's palm, a bill at a time.

"One hundred, two hundred, three hundred, four—" Madame Bovary counted them off, her face lit by raw greed. She squealed like a child being given a fond birthday wish as he continued adding to the pile until she reached one thousand.

"More than enough, I should hazard," Ellery said, replacing the rest.

Madame Bovary raised the money to her nose and sniffed them, as if the bills were a fragrant bouquet. "My dearest Ellery, feel free to rouse me from sleep anytime your heart desires."

Venus had observed the transaction in wonderment. "What about me?" she asked. "I helped too."

"That you did," Ellery said. "Here's another hundred just for you."

"A measly hundred?" Venus complained as she accepted the bill. "Bovary got more than I earn in a year!"

For the third time that night, Lou was witness to the awful change that could come over Worthington at the slightest provocation. He rounded on the soiled angel and viciously backhanded her across the face. Venus stumbled against the wall and raised an arm to shield herself as Ellery went to hit her again. But it was Madame Bovary who stopped him by inserting herself between them.

"Here, now! I won't have any of that! I don't care if you have more money than Midas, I won't let you hurt this poor girl."

The dapper dandy controlled his temper with a visible effort. Lowering his hand, he glowered a moment, then wheeled. "We've wasted enough time, gentlemen. Let's enjoy ourselves while the night is still young."

Teddy Payne gripped Louisa's wrist. "That's your cue, girl. You're in for an experience you'll never forget."

Lou resisted. "What about my buckskins and other things?" Her rifle and pistols had been deposited on a corner table, and she would dearly love to get her hands on either.

"Bovary will look after everything," Bellows said. "After we're done with you, you can come back for them."

"After," Payne emphasized, and tittered.

As the door swung shut behind them, Lou glanced back to see Madame Bovary comforting Venus, who was bawling like a child, the imprint of Ellery's palm flame-red on her cheek. Without thinking, Lou remarked, "Your friend is a brute."

Payne was swaggering along, swinging his mahogany cane. "Ellery? Oh, hardly. Yes, he can be a trifle touchy if he's crossed. But by and large he has the most genial of dispositions."

Bellows was behind them, his hands shoved into his pockets. "Don't do anything to antagonize him and you'll be fine."

Ellery was up ahead, at a street corner, impatiently tapping his foot. "The Golden Bough or the Scarlet Lady. Which will it be?"

"The Golden Bough," Payne said.

"The Scarlet Lady" was Bellows's choice.

"Which leaves it up to me," Ellery said, and bore to the

124

left. He began to hum to himself. Many of the women who were abroad gave him second looks, as well they should. For all his faults, Ellery Quinton Worthington was a remarkably handsome rogue, and knew it. He flaunted his looks, walking with an exaggerated sway, his dancing eyes undressing every attractive female.

Payne had relaxed his hold on Lou but still had her by the wrist. "Ahhh, now the fun begins," he said. "Nightlife gets into a person's blood. It's like a potent drug. All the excitement, the thrills."

"The more you have, the more you want," Bellows clarified.

Lou was becoming conscious of stares directed her way and couldn't make up her mind whether to be flattered or offended. "Give me a quiet night in the Rockies any day."

Bellows came up alongside her. "What's so special about the mountains?"

"They are a world unto themselves, so high they brush the clouds," Lou said longingly. "At night you can hear wolves howl, coyotes yip, and painters scream. Sometimes for hours on end."

"You'd prefer that to this?" Payne said, motioning at the crowded thoroughfare with its gaily dressed people and flow of clattering carriages. "You really *are* a little savage, aren't you?"

"To each their own," Lou said archly.

Payne doffed his hat to a trio of lovelies. "Give me a strong drink, the rustle of silk, the tinkle of a woman's laugh any day."

Bellows joined in. "The scent of perfume, the smell of a good cigar, the joy of cleaning out another man at cards."

"Exactly," Payne said. "What are wolf farts and coyote belches compared to the marvelous benefits of civilization?"

"You'd never understand," Lou said.

"Nor would I want to," Payne told her. "I was born to be a rake and a scoundrel, and I make no apologies about it to anyone."

"Same here," Bellows said. "Except I do apologize to my father from time to time when I step too far out of bounds. I have the family inheritance to think of, after all."

Both men laughed, which caused Ellery to slow down until they caught up. "It's nice to see everyone in fine spirits again. To keep you happy, I'll buy the first round tonight."

"What a saint!" Payne said.

Another block brought them to a stately building Lou would never have suspected of being a den of iniquity. Stone steps climbed to wide wooden doors. The interior was as opulent as a sultan's harem, with thick carpet and tapestries and furniture polished to a sheen. Games of chance were the main attraction. She saw so many gold necklaces and rings, she lost count.

"The Scarlet Lady," Ellery said. "Consider yourself honored, wench. It's one of the premier clubs in all of St. Louis. Members only, and their guests."

"And memberships cost five hundred dollars a year," Bellows mentioned.

A balding man in his fifties rushed to meet them, wearing an immaculate brown jacket and pants. Lou saw others wearing the same and concluded they must work there.

"Mr. Worthington! Mr. Payne! Mr. Bellows! How splendid of you to grace us with a visit."

Ellery gave his hat to the man but retained his cane. "Good evening, Slattersby. We'd like our usual table. And a bottle brought, posthaste." He indicated Lou. "We'd also like you to meet our guest. Miss Louisa May Clark, of the famous Boston Clarks. Her family made their fortune in shipping, in the Orient. Spices and furs and what have you."

"You don't say?" Slattersby said, giving a slight bow.

Lou opened her mouth to retract Ellery's false claims, but Payne squeezed her wrist in subtle warning.

"Treat the young lady as you would one of us," Ellery said. "Her every wish should be your command."

"Without hesitation, sir," Slattersby dutifully responded.

"Excellent." Ellery clasped Lou's hand and steered her toward the head of the enormous room. "I saw that," he said crisply. "Spoil our entertainment, my dear, and it will go hard on you. Very hard indeed."

"You made that whole story up."

"Your point?"

"That it's not nice to go around spreading lies."

Ellery stopped and stared at her. "You really believe that, don't you? What a dull life you must live. Tomorrow you should hie yourself to a nunnery and spend the rest of your days in a convent, protected from the real world."

Lou was tempted to give Ellery a piece of her mind, but just then a dashing male patron happened to walk by, his gaze lingering on her as if she were a full water skin and he had just spent a week in a parched desert. The only other man who had ever looked at her like that was Zach, and it startled her so much, it rendered her speechless.

Ellery headed for an empty table. Beside it was another, ringed by people playing cards. "As I live and breathe," he declared, "this is your lucky night, girl. See that gentleman in the silver cravat? If he takes an interest in you, your future is assured."

"Who is he?" Lou absently asked. She really didn't care.

"One of the most powerful men in the city. His name is Festerman. Lon Festerman."

Chapter Ten

For over an hour Zach King sat and watched masters of the game of poker play hand after hand, and in that hour he learned more about the game than he had learned in the preceding eighteen years of his life.

Try as Zach might, he could never tell whether a player's hand was good or bad. LeBeau, Carson, and the rest never gave a hint. Their faces were blank slates when they were dealt cards, and whenever they looked at their hands they adopted stony expressions. They wagered with immense skill, bluffing when it suited them, folding when it fitted their strategy, and often winning big.

Adam Tyler, though, didn't sit in. He sat facing the doorway, waiting. Zach leaned against a wall, too agitated to sit down. He was so jumpy that whenever anyone entered the room his hands dropped to the expensive pistols Tyler had given him.

Henri LeBeau won the latest pot and swept in the pile of chips with gleeful relish. "My fine friends!" he declared.

"Keep giving me your money at this rate and I will be able to afford to retire."

Carson made puffing noises. "The only thing worse than a poor loser is a poor winner," he commented dryly.

Everyone, even Zach, laughed. Everyone except Adam Tyler. The tall gambler rose, stretched, and said, "I'm going to ask around. I'll be back in a bit."

No sooner had Tyler departed than LeBeau swung toward Zach with a speed belying his great size. "Give us the whole story, *vite*. We only have a few minutes."

Zach hesitated. He had an ingrained reluctance to talk about his personal life, and a strong hunch Adam Tyler might not approve. "I don't know—"

Carson scowled and rapped his fingers on the table. "We're not *asking* you, boy, we're *telling* you. Tyler is a friend of ours, and we don't want him to come to any harm. Just give us the essentials, enough for us to fully appreciate what he's involved in."

After all Tyler had done for him, Zach reflected, it was only fair. So, briefly and to the point, he related the sequence of events, from the incident at Sylvia Banner's to his fight with the two rivermen.

"Lost puppies and kittens," LeBeau said when Zach finished. "It is always so with Adam, *non*?"

Carson pushed erect. "We can't let his noble sentiments bury him. I'll spread the word. From here on out, we'll keep an eye on him and be ready."

LeBeau nodded. "The brotherhood does not let down its own."

"What brotherhood?" Zach asked as Carson hurried out.

The Frenchman sipped some port before answering. "It is—how would you say?—a fraternity, my young friend. A brotherhood, if you will, of the best gamblers in the city." He took another sip. "By nature we are loners, by profession we are competitors. In a game of chance we are always at each other's throat. But when a common enemy rears, we are brothers united. *Comprendez-vous*?"

Zach knew a little French, courtesy of the voyagers he had met in the mountains. "Yes, I understand. It's the same with my people, the Shoshones. Attack one, and you attack us all."

"Your people?" LeBeau said. "You think of yourself as Indian only?"

"Let's just say I'm not as fond of my white blood as I am of my Shoshone blood."

LeBeau cocked his head. "Why? Didn't you mention that your *pere,* your papa, is white? Is he of no account?"

"My pa?" Zach was insulted. "He's the most decent man I know."

"Then it seems to me that not all white blood is bad, eh? It is your life, monsieur, and you are free to do as you want, but to deny half your heritage is to deny half of what makes you who you are. That would be a grave mistake. And make your papa very sad, *non*?" LeBeau faced the table. "But enough chitchat. We must not let Adam suspect." Scooping up the cards, he shuffled and dealt.

Zach pondered the Frenchman's advice. To be honest, he'd never given any thought to how his father would be affected by his attitude toward whites. He'd always assumed his father would understand and forgive him.

Zach had to admit that not all whites were wicked. Adam Tyler was decent; the gambler was risking his life to help a stranger. The same applied to George Milhouse. And there were other whites, men like Shakespeare McNair, Scott Kendall, and Jim Bridger, who had always treated Zach exactly as they treated everyone else. If there were more whites like them, Zach mused, the world would be a much better place.

Tyler returned and crooked a finger. "We're leaving. Worthington and his friends haven't shown up, so we'll make the rounds of a few likely spots."

"Want some company, *mon ami*?" LeBeau asked.

"I thank you, but no," Tyler replied. "I don't want to drag anyone else into this. It's mine to do, and mine alone."

"As you wish," the Frenchman said. Only Zach noticed the sly grin that split LaBeau's features.

Several men in dark frock coats and wide-brimmed hats were lounging at the entrance to the Golden Bough. Two of them, Zach observed, trailed Tyler and him out. After a few blocks the pair blended into the shadows, only to be replaced by two more.

Zach admired these men. The gambling fraternity was taking care of its own, doing much as Shoshones would do. He glimpsed others occasionally, dark men in dark clothes who blended so well into the night that spotting them was difficult.

Tyler's next stop was a gambling house called the Tiger's Den, a reference, no doubt, to faro, where players wagered on cards kept in a dealer's box that was usually decorated with the image of a tiger. Zach found himself becoming more and more fascinated by the various games. He toyed with the idea of trying his hand at one or two after Louisa was safe.

They didn't find her at the Tiger's Den. They didn't find her at the Baldwin House, nor at the Delta Club. Zach began to despair of ever seeing his beloved again, and regretted not scouring the city on his own earlier. They had wasted too much time in going to Tyler's and having him change clothes, time better spent searching.

Everywhere they went, Zach saw men in frock coats and black hats. He could never quite be sure which of them were keeping an eye on Adam Tyler and which were merely going about their own business.

"I'm sorry, son," the tall gambler said as they hastened toward yet another haven for the city's well-to-do. "I was confident we'd find your fiancée by now."

"I'll do it if it takes a year," Zach vowed, and meant it. He wouldn't leave St. Louis as long as Lou was missing. If he had to, he would rent a room. He had enough money to last a couple of months, courtesy of his father. After that, he would take a job to make ends meet and spend his off hours constantly hunting.

"We're not licked yet," Tyler said. "A few coins in the right palms, a few words in the right ears, and half the footpads and river rats in the city will be out looking for her. It's only a matter of time before you're reunited."

Zach made bold to ask a question that had been gnawing at him for hours. "Why are you doing this?"

"I knew your father, remember."

"Not well enough to risk your life." Zach was prying where he shouldn't. It might annoy the older man, but Zach had to know.

The man in black bowed his head. His face was shrouded in the brim of his hat as he said, "The way you talk about your fiancée makes it plain you love her very much."

"Yes. So?"

"So I loved someone once. Her name was Mary. She was the daughter of a cotton king, and I worshiped the ground she walked on."

"Where is she now?"

"I lost her."

It was a whisper. "How?" Zach inquired.

For over a minute Tyler didn't answer. Zach figured he was going to and let it drop. Then Tyler cleared his throat.

"I was about your age. My father and I lived in the bayou country on a small plot of land. The cotton king was our neighbor, and he tended to look down his nose at anyone who had less money than he did. Mary was his daughter." Tyler smiled. "From the moment I laid eyes on her, I loved her. She was the only one for me, if that makes sense to you."

Zach thought of Louisa. "It does."

"Mary felt the same, it turned out. We spent every spare moment together for months on end. We talked of becoming engaged, of getting married, of rearing a family of our own. It was our dream. A dream her father didn't share. One day I came to court her and he had me thrown off their estate after informing me I wasn't good enough for any daughter of his." Resentment choked Tyler off. Taking a deep breath, he continued. "That didn't stop us, though. We met in secret for months, biding our time while I saved every penny I could get my hands on. We had made up our minds to elope. Once we were married, there wasn't a thing her father could do."

Tyler was so intent on his story that he nearly collided with a man coming around a corner.

"Why don't you watch where you're walking, damn you?"

Adam Tyler looked up. Something in his eyes made the other man retreat a step, then walk wide to the left to avoid them.

"No, sir. No, sir," the man said. "I didn't mean anything. It's been a long day, is all. Go your way in peace, and I'll go mine." Pivoting, he ran off.

Tyler had already forgotten him. "You should have seen her, Zach. How happy Mary was. Her sweet smile, her beauty. The love in her eyes for me. She was every man's dream come true. All I could ever want, and more. Soul mates, she called us, and it fit. Our rightful destiny was to spend the rest of our lives together, to grow old side by side, to live our love to its fullest."

Again Zach was reminded of Lou.

"But her father thought differently. He had his servants spy on her. He learned about our secret meetings. And on the eve of the night we were to elope, he sent hired thugs to my father's farm. My father had no idea who they were and walked out to greet them." Tyler halted and put a hand to his brow. "They beat him to death with clubs."

A pair of ladies were strolling by. One started to come toward them, saying, "Are you all right, mister?" Zach waved them on.

"I was inside, packing to leave." The man in black resumed walking. "I heard my father yell and ran to the door. When I saw the men, I knew. God help me, I knew. I

133

grabbed a pair of pistols and killed three of them before they reached the house, then I barred the door and held them off. But they didn't give up. They were under orders. They set fire to the stable and the outbuildings, then to the farmhouse itself."

Zach was hanging on every word.

"Flames leaped to the sky. They could be seen for miles. Mary saw them, and with no thought for her own safety she jumped on her mare and raced to our place." Tyler talked faster, as if forcing the rest out. "She came galloping out of the night, screaming my name. In all the noise and confusion, one of the men her father hired didn't realize who she was. Maybe he thought she was kin of mine. She was wearing a cloak with a hood—" The gambler coughed. "The thug shot her. When they realized what they had done, they panicked and ran off. I was frantic. I rushed out and held her in my arms as she died. Her last words were, 'I'll always love you.' Then she was gone."

"I'm sorry," Zach said huskily. His own throat had a lump in it.

"I cried and cried," Tyler said, "while our farm burned down around me. At dawn I buried her and my father, side by side, on a knoll where she and I used to picnic. All I had left in the world were two pistols and the clothes on my back. I left."

"What about her father?"

"He's still alive."

"You never made him pay for what he did?"

Tyler tilted his face to the stars. "I wanted to. God, how I wanted to. But I knew I would be throwing my life away if I went to his plantation alone. So I rode off, thinking to bide my time and come back one day. But later I learned he'd sold his property and left. Everyone said it was because he was crushed by Mary's death."

"Do you know where he is now?"

"Yes. I've known for some time. But I haven't confronted him. I've made excuses not to. I convinced myself

134

I didn't want to dredge up the past, dredge up all that pain. It still gives me nightmares after all these years." Tyler slowed. "I was deluding myself. I see that now, thanks to you."

"Me?"

"Every fire needs a spark to start, and you're the spark that's started mine burning again."

Zach was totally perplexed. "You're making no sense. I haven't done anything. You're the one going out of his way to help a perfect stranger."

"It was fate that brought us together, son. Fate, giving me a kick on the backside. Giving me a sign that the time has come." Tyler sighed. "No one can escape their past."

"You've lost me," Zach said.

Across the street loomed a stately building with a most unusual name: the Scarlet Lady. Tyler turned toward it, then stopped and faced around. "You deserve to know the rest of it. Mary's father was never the best of men, but he became much worse after she was gone. His wife had died giving birth to her, so he had no one else. He took to womanizing and gambling. With the money he had, he set up his own little empire. An empire of vice and pleasure on demand. He turned an entire city into his personal hell." Adam Tyler paused. "This city."

"St. Louis?"

Tyler placed his hands on Zach's shoulders. "You haven't guessed yet? My young friend, Mary's full name was Mary Louise Festerman."

"Festerman? Then Lon is—!"

"Her father."

Zach didn't know what to say.

"When you told me how Sylvia Banner tried to abduct Louisa and turn her over to Festerman, something snapped inside of me. I knew he was vile, but I didn't know *how* vile. I didn't know he was forcing young women into a life of ill repute." Tyler walked toward the Scarlet Lady. "I can't make excuses any longer. Lon must be stopped. And stop him I will, or die trying."

Zach was deep in thought as they climbed stone stairs and mingled with more lavishly adorned women and immaculate gentlemen. Now he knew the real reason the gambler was helping him. It had little to do with Lou. Tyler's motives were personal. Yet it didn't matter as long as the end result was the same, as long as Lou was rescued and back in his arms where she belonged.

Suddenly the man in black stopped. He did it so abruptly that Zach couldn't help bumping into him, but Tyler didn't complain. The gambler was staring hawk-eyed at three young men seated at a table at the front of the room. Zach felt a tingle shoot through him. Without being told, he knew it was Worthington and Worthington's two friends. His heart sank when he saw Louisa wasn't with them, and he began to move past Tyler to learn where she was.

"No," Tyler said, thrusting an arm in front of him. "Stay out of sight. They might recognize you and bolt." Holding his right arm bent at the elbow close to his waist, Tyler walked up to their table and nodded at each of them in turn. "Ellery Worthington. Eddy Payne. Reggie Bellows. Just when I'd given up hope."

Zach realized Tyler had identified them for his benefit, so he would know who was who. Slipping behind a roulette wheel, he rested his hands on the polished butts of his pistols.

The three dandies had glanced up in surprise. "Adam Tyler?" Worthington said. "I don't believe we've seen you since that game at the Imperial eight or nine weeks ago."

Eddy Payne was regarding the gambler with ill-concealed contempt. "Where you took us for every dollar we had, as I recall."

"It was a fair game," Tyler said flatly.

Bellows straightened. "Oh, we'd never imply otherwise. Everyone knows you're as honest as they come. Which is more than can be said for two-thirds of the gamblers in this city."

Tyler moved to the right. "A true gentleman should

always put honesty above all else. Some might say it's stupid for someone in my profession to place such a high premium on honor, but without honor we're no better than the beasts in the swamps."

Ellery laughed. "Why, who would have guessed you have a philosophical bent? So do I, when the mood strikes. We're a lot alike."

"We're nothing alike," Tyler said, each syllable as clipped and precise as the strokes of an ax.

Zach saw the younger men stiffen. They sensed something was wrong, but they had no notion what it might be.

"I could construe that as an insult," Ellery said.

"Construe it any way you like" was Tyler's harsh rejoinder.

They caught on, then. They knew he was deliberately prodding them, and they didn't like it. Payne squirmed like a worm on a hook, Ellery flushed like a beet, while Bellows slowly laid his hands on the tablecloth, his fingers splayed.

"Have we somehow offended you, Mr. Tyler?"

"Your very existence is an offense," the man in black answered. "You were reared in the lap of luxury. You could have made a difference in the world, could have done something to make it better. Instead, you squander your wealth and your talents in endless debauchery."

Ellery gripped the edge of the table so hard, his knuckles were pale. "And I suppose you're perfect? Since when does a *gambler* lecture others about the value of the lives they lead? You're overstepping the line, mister, and you'd damn well better rein in your claws."

"Or what?" Tyler said.

The gauntlet had been thrown, and for tense seconds the three dandies were as motionless as statues. People nearby had overheard and were prudently moving elsewhere. Whispers spread like wildfire.

"I asked you a question," Tyler goaded.

Bellows had more common sense than the other two combined. "We don't want any trouble," he said civilly. "We're minding our own business, and we'd admire if you did the same."

Tyler lowered his right wrist and it lightly rapped the table. A heavy thump hinted there was more up his sleeve than flesh and bone. "Earlier tonight you grabbed a young woman off the street. What happened to her?"

"The little savage?" Payne said. "What's she to you?"

"Where is she?" Tyler pressed them.

Ellery's hand was inching toward his jacket. "You have some gall, gambler. Maybe you've forgotten who you're dealing with. My father could chew you up and spit you out without working up a sweat."

"Your father isn't here. You are."

Payne had stopped squirming and was leaning back. "Are you drunk, Tyler? Is that it? You've had too much whiskey and don't know what you're saying? Because no one in their right mind would incur the wrath of our families."

"Not that we want to incur your wrath, either," Bellows quickly said. "We hold you no ill will. If you'd explain what this is all about, we might be able to accommodate you. Is that too much to ask?"

Zach was afraid Tyler would refuse, that the gambler would kill all three before learning where Lou was. On an impulse he stepped to the gambler's side, saying, "It's about my fiancée. What have you done with her?"

Shock immobilized Bellows. Payne gawked as if beholding a pink alligator. Ellery alone was unfazed, a vicious gleam creeping into his cold eyes. "So. The half-breed. And dressed like a gentleman born and bred."

"It's an insult," Payne said. "He has no more right in here than a slug. Call Slattersby and have him thrown out."

Adam Tyler wagged a finger. "I wouldn't, were I you."

"All we want is my fiancée," Zach said. But he wanted much more. He wanted to bash in their skulls with a war club. He wanted to gut them. To slit their throats. To take their scalps and attach them to his coup stick. He wanted them to suffer. But they were his only link to Lou, and he couldn't touch them.

Ellery sneered. "Obviously she's not with us."

"She was," Tyler said. "Where is she now?"

"Why should we tell you?" Ellery arrogantly demanded.

"Because if you don't, you won't live out the night," the man in black said in the same arrogant tone.

"You wouldn't dare," Ellery mocked him.

Bellows was glancing right and left and growing as white as a sheet. "Don't do anything rash," he cautioned.

Zach, too, had seen dark men in dark frock coats sprout like stalks of corn on all sides, some close at hand, some farther off. Grimly silent, they hovered like birds of prey awaiting the signal to swoop down.

Grinning savagely, Ellery heaved up out of his chair, flinging it to the floor behind him. Coiled like a viper, he glared at Adam Tyler. "You don't scare me, mister. I've always said your reputation was overblown, and now I'll prove it."

"Don't!" Bellows cried, but his friends ignored him.

"You're a fool, Worthington," Tyler said gravely. "Money doesn't make a man invincible."

Zach was hoping to avoid bloodshed. Somehow, some way, he must convince everyone to stay calm, at least until he discovered where Lou was. But then he saw Ellery's features twist into a feral mask, and his stomach churned. It was too late to reason with them. It was too late for anything except what happened next.

Ellery Quinton Worthington the Third stabbed a hand under his jacket and swept it out holding a pistol. He was smiling, confident of his speed, his prowess.

Instantly, Adam Tyler's right arm snapped forward and a gleaming derringer blossomed in his palm. It cracked loud and sharp, spewing smoke and lead. Above Worthington's nose a new hole appeared.

Simultaneously, Eddy Payne produced a pistol and pushed upward, but he never made it to his feet.

Zach was unlimbering his own flintlocks. He would have beaten Payne, but others had already taken aim. A thunderous volley tore into both Payne and Worthington, ripping them to pieces, jolting them backward into crumpled, pathetic heaps. The dark men in their dark coats each fired once, then melted into the crowd like the wisps of smoke from their weapons. They were there one instant, gone the next.

Only Bellows was untouched, frozen in horror, his hands still splayed on the table.

Adam Tyler pointed the derringer at him. "Last chance. What have you done with Louisa May Clark?"

"She's gone!" Bellows bleated. "He took her! She didn't want to go with him, but there was nothing she could do!"

"Who?" Zach asked.

"Festerman. Lon Festerman."

Chapter Eleven

When Louisa May Clark was a little girl her parents took her one summer to visit a distant relative, a cousin of her father's, a farmer who owned two hundred and fifty acres of prime bottomland. They spent two weeks on the farm, two of the worst weeks of Louisa's childhood.

Things had gotten off to a bad start when she was attacked by several geese the moment she climbed down from the wagon. The geese had come honking and flapping at her as if she were a coyote out to eat them. Terrified, she had cringed against a wheel and one of them had pecked her before the farmer shooed them off. Her mother had calmed her, and then the adults shared a laugh at how scared she had been.

Lou hadn't thought it was so funny. Nor did she like how the farmer's frisky dog kept nipping at her heels, or how the big red rooster always took it on himself to chase her out of the barnyard.

But the worst part of the visit had been Mad Gus. Shortly after they arrived, the farmer had mentioned to her that she had the run of his place. She could go anywhere she pleased, do anything she wanted, *except* go near the pen at the back of the barn. Under no circumstances was she to venture anywhere near it. When she asked why, the farmer told her that the pen was home to his bull, Mad Gus. Gus was used for breeding, and he was worth a lot of money. He was also the meanest bull who ever lived. He always tried to gore or trample anyone who came near him, except for the farmer.

Over the course of the next few days, Lou had learned more about Gus. How he had severely hurt a worker once, nearly killing him. How he had trampled one of the farmer's chickens to death when it strayed into his pen.

The stories filled Lou with fear. In her mind she pictured Mad Gus as a four-legged ogre. He was as tall as a tree and bulging with muscles. She pictured him as always foaming at the mouth, always stomping and pawing and snorting. He had great six-foot horns, which he constantly swung to and fro in his eagerness to rend and maim. The mere mention of his name sent chills down her spine.

Yet despite being scared, Lou was curious. Each day she would muster her courage and walk toward the back of the barn to take a peek at the pen, but each day fright stopped her before she reached the corner.

It wasn't until the last day of the family's stay that Lou wrestled with her fear and won, and then only because she realized it was her last chance. If she didn't get a peek at Mad Gus then, she never would.

Every nerve atingle, Lou crept to the barn and peered past. After all she had heard, after all she had imagined, she felt sure the ground would shake from Mad Gus's hooves and the air would be filled with the foul stench of his fetid breath. Instead, the air smelled of apples from a nearby orchard, and all was quiet except for the merry singing of birds.

In the pen stood a very ordinary old bull dozing in the heat of the midday sun. Mad Gus wasn't any taller than a horse. His horns were short, his body drooped. His ears lazily flicked at circling flies. All in all, he was about the least scariest animal Lou had ever seen. The geese and the big red rooster were scarier.

Lou had gone farther, forcing her legs to take her to the pen. She'd stood next to the rails and said, "So you're Mad Gus?"

The bull had turned his sleepy eyes toward her. Lou tensed, thinking it would roar and charge. She envisioned it breaking through the pen and stomping her. But all Mad Gus did was grunt. That was it. He grunted, and ignored her.

Lou never forgot the lesson she learned on that farm. How fear mostly came from within a person. How it was possible to so build up things in her head to where she saw monsters where none existed.

Now she was reminded of that lesson once again. For ever since Lou had heard Lon Festerman mentioned, she had imagined the vilest of human scum, a huge, hulking brute of a man, ugly in body as well as soul, so vicious that he had people murdered at the snap of a finger. In her mind she pictured a savage face twisted by hate, the eyes aglow with raw lust and a craving for violence.

Instead, at the next table sat an ordinary-looking man in his fifties. He was no taller than Zach, his shoulders slightly bent, his frame lean, his face soft, almost gentle in its expression. Streaks of gray ran through his hair. He looked for all the world like someone's kindly old grandfather.

This was the scourge of St. Louis? Lou thought to herself, and almost laughed aloud. At Festerman's elbow was an attractive woman in a tight red dress. Behind them, ringing Festerman's chair, were three beefy characters. Bodyguards, Lou reckoned.

"I'm going to say hi," Ellery Worthington declared.

Bellows gripped his friend's arm. "Why bother him? You know how he can be at times. Leave well enough alone."

"Don't tell me you're afraid?" Ellery taunted. He moved

toward the other table, toward Festerman, only to be brought up short by one of the bodyguards, who stepped in front of him and put a hand on his chest.

"That's far enough."

"Out of my way, flunky," Ellery snapped.

The bodyguard stayed where he was. "Boss?"

Lon Festerman idly glanced around. He was slouched in his chair and wore a look of bored indifference to the game of cards he was playing and the world in general. "Ah. Mr. Worthington. Out on one of your nightly revels?" His voice didn't grate like steel on a grindstone, as Lou had expected. It was as ordinary as the rest of him. "Let the boy by, Vance."

The husky bodyguard obeyed.

Everyone had stopped playing to watch. Ellery enjoyed being the center of attention and strutted up to Festerman's chair. "Nice to see you again, Lon. I hear you've opened a new house down on Hanover Street. I plan to pay it a visit soon."

Lou saw Festerman's jaw muscles twitch.

"Have you also heard that familiarity breeds contempt? Strange that I don't recall giving you permission to address me by my first name."

Ellery deflated a little. "Oh, come on. How long have we known each other? You've been to our house half a dozen times."

"On business with your father," Festerman said. Sighing, he looked at the lovely woman beside him. "Did you hear this upstart, Stephanie? He's a living example of one of the main problems in our world today. Lack of respect for one's elders."

"That's not true," Ellery said. "There's no one in the world I respect more than I respect you."

Festerman didn't seem to hear him. "Young people, Stephanie, think they have the God-given right to do as they damn well please. Even when a parent knows what is best for them, they'll rebel and go their own way. A father can talk himself blue and it won't do any good. Fools and the young rush headlong into tragedy, I've learned."

Ellery began to slowly back away.

"As for you," Festerman swung toward him, "if it wasn't for my friendship with your father, I'd have you taken out back and horsewhipped. Spare the rod and spoil the child. I should know. I was too lenient once, and I paid for my neglect with the greatest loss any parent can endure."

"Sir?" Ellery said.

Festerman gave a toss of his head and dropped his cards on the table. "We've been here long enough. Cash in my winnings, Stephanie. We're leaving." He rose, and instantly one of his bodyguards produced a coat, hat, and cane. Festerman started to slip an arm into the coat swiveling as he did.

Lou's skin prickled. He had seen her. He paused, a gleam entering his eyes, as if matches had been lit inside them. Waving the bodyguard aside, he brushed past Ellery and sauntered over to her.

"What have we here?"

Bellows answered. "Allow me to introduce Louisa May Clark, Mr. Festerman, sir. An acquaintance of ours."

"You don't say?" Festerman tore his gaze from Lou. "Ah, Mr. Bellows and Mr. Payne. Forgive my rudeness. Mind if I join you?" Before either could reply, he swept out a chair and indicated Lou should sit. "For you, my dear, since neither of these bumpkins has seen fit to be a proper gentleman."

Although she would just as soon pick up the chair and hit him with it, Lou did as she was bid.

Festerman pulled out the chair next to hers, contriving to sit so that his shoulder brushed hers. Lou slid back a trifle so they weren't touching, and Festerman smiled. "I've never seen you before. You must be newly arrived in St. Louis, or else you've been hiding under a bushel. I'd never forget one so lovely."

Eddy Payne lowered himself into a seat across from them. Lou saw him grin and wink at Bellows, who shook his head. Payne leaned forward. "She's from Boston, sir. Her family made their money in the Orient."

"Is that so?" Festerman said offhandedly.

David Thompson

Lou had had enough of their lies. "No, it isn't. My fiancée and I just got into the city this morning." To her it seemed as if they had ridden in ages before. "We live in the Rockies."

Lon Festerman turned toward Eddy Payne. "Then what was that nonsense about the Orient?"

"It's a game they're playing," Lou said. "Seeing how many people they can fool. They bought this dress for me. I couldn't afford it in a million years." She derived immense delight from the stark fear abruptly mirrored by Payne and Bellows. At last she was giving them a taste of their own medicine.

"Do my ears deceive me?" Festerman said to Eddy Payne. "You have the gall to try and make a fool out of *me*?" He snapped his fingers.

Suddenly the three bodyguards were there, two with hands under their jackets, the husky one, Vance, standing behind Payne with his big fists balled.

Ellery darted over, quickly saying, "He didn't mean to offend you, Mr. Festerman. Honest. He's just had a little too much to drink and forgot who he was talking to."

Lou was relishing her triumph. "Another lie. They haven't had a drink since I met them, hours ago."

Ellery jabbed a finger at her. "Stay out of this!"

Festerman nodded at Vance, who pivoted and drove his right fist into the pit of Ellery's stomach. Ellery folded in half, spitting and sucking in air, and Vance slammed him into a chair.

"Now, then," Festerman said icily, "suppose the young lady tells me exactly what this is all about."

All too glad to, Lou related her encounter. She deliberately refrained from saying anything about Zach and made no mention of her harrowing ordeal at Sylvia Banner's.

Storm clouds brewed on Festerman's brow. When she was done, he smoothed his silver cravat, then smiled thinly at Ellery, Payne, and Bellows. "So. You were trying to dupe me. Me, of all people. Your antics are well known to me, boys, but I never conceived you would be so crass. It's an insult of monumental proportions."

Ellery's skin had grown pasty. "The last thing we'd ever want to do is insult you, Mr. Festerman. Honest."

"You wouldn't know what honesty is if it jumped up and bit you on the ass," Festerman said, then bobbed his chin at Lou. "I apologize for my crude language. But I won't brook such insolence. I should have them chained and thrown in the Mississippi."

"You wouldn't dare!" Ellery declared. "My father would . . ."

"Would *what*?" Festerman snarled with such vehemence, the dandies wilted like flowers in a hailstorm. "Do you really believe your father would challenge *me*? Unlike you, he is a man of intelligence and refinement. He knows I could crush him as easily as I'd crush a flea."

"You're crazy," Ellery responded.

Lon Festerman barked a command at Vance, and the burly bodyguard's right hand clamped onto Ellery throat and squeezed. Ellery resisted, prying at Vance's thick fingers and hitting the bodyguard's thick arm, but he might as well have been hitting a tree limb. Vance kept squeezing until Ellery was nearly unconscious and moving as sluggishly as a snail.

"Release the simpleton," Festerman ordered.

Ellery slumped onto the table. His lips moved, but no sounds came out. Spittle dribbled over his lower lip onto the cloth.

"Out of respect for your father I will forgive tonight's stupidity," Festerman announced. "But be advised that none of you are ever again to speak to me in public unless I speak to you first. If you do, I will have your tongues cut out." Rising, Festerman extended his hand to Lou. "And now, my dear, I would be honored if you would accompany me." He glanced archly at Ellery. "Unless you have an objection, Mr. Worthington?"

"No," Ellery wheezed. "No, sir."

"I didn't think so."

Lou, though, had no intention of going anywhere. The stories told about Lon Festerman were true. Appearances, as the old saying went, could be deceiving. His kindly exterior masked a core of unbounded cruelty. "If it's all the same to you," she said sweetly, "I have business of my own to tend to."

"Business that can wait," Festerman said. He raised his arms, and his coat materialized. "I insist that you join me."

Lou noticed that everyone within earshot was doing their best to act indifferent to what transpired. They were afraid, and rightfully so. "Please," she said. "I must go find my fiancé."

Eddy Payne, who had been cowed into silence, chose that moment to vent his spite. "A miserable half-breed!" he muttered.

"Explain yourself," Festerman instructed him.

"Her fiancé is part Indian. Last we saw, he was fighting a couple of rivermen. Typical breed." Payne smirked at her. "What a waste! A fine white girl like her, marrying a mongrel heathen. I'm surprised her father and mother would let her."

"My folks are dead," Lou declared.

Festerman nodded knowingly. "And without their guidance, your morals have lapsed. You let the half-breed take advantage of you."

Rising anger made Lou careless. "No one has ever taken advantage of me!" she responded, and realized her mistake when a new gleam came into Festerman's dark eyes, a hungry sort of gleam that had nothing to do with food.

"You don't say?"

"I'd like to go," Lou stressed, and turned. Immediately, the other two bodyguards were on either side of her, holding her arms.

Festerman donned his hat. "My dear, you must become versed in the social graces. When someone courteously requests the pleasure of your company, have the decency to humor them."

In short order, Louisa had been ushered from the Scarlet Lady and to a waiting row of carriages. The largest and most elegant, a six-seat landau with a leather top, belonged to Festerman. A footman held Lou's hand while she stepped up, then Festerman sat across from her. Stephanie started to enter, but he told her to ride with Vance and the other bodyguards.

As the landau rolled into motion, Lou peered over a shoulder through a glass panel and saw the others climbing into a victoria.

Festerman patted the smooth seat. "Moroccan upholstery. Glass sides. Folding bow tops. They don't come any finer."

"Are you trying to impress me?" Lou asked.

"A man would need to be an idiot not to want to make a favorable impression on someone so beautiful."

"Then how many grizzlies have you killed? How many coup have you counted?"

"You're serious? Apparently you've lived in the mountains much too long, young lady. You need refining."

"I need to be let out right this second and allowed to go my own way," Lou said.

"I'm sorry, little one, but that's quite out of the question. In case you haven't noticed, I'm accustomed to doing as I please. And it pleases me to have you be my companion for the foreseeable future."

"Even if I don't want to be?"

"Your personal feelings are irrelevant." Festerman gazed out the window at the flow of nightgoers. "See all those good people? I'm lord of them all. I am the single most powerful person in all of St. Louis."

"Bragging is awful childish," Lou remarked. "Something I'd expect from Ellery and his friends."

Festerman didn't take offense at the slight. "My dear girl, I was merely stating a fact. Tonight you have entered into a whole new realm. An arena of power and wealth such as your young mind can't comprehend."

Lou had to admit the man was a bundle of surprises. She'd figured he would be a crude, vulgar brute, yet he was cultured and debonair. "I reckon I comprehend a lot more than you give me credit for."

"Touché," Festerman said, and laughed. "You and I will have superb times together. Tonight you'll be my guest, then tomorrow we'll go shopping for—"

"Hold your horses," Lou said. "I'm not staying the night at your place, tonight or any other night."

"Where else would you stay? Do you have a hotel room?"

"No," Lou admitted, and promptly regretted it.

"There you go. I'd be terribly remiss if I failed to offer you the hospitality of my humble home."

Lou found out exactly how "humble" his home was when the landau pulled up in front of a wrought-iron gate set in a high stone wall. Two men carrying shotguns opened it, and the team of white horses pulled the landau up a winding, tree-lined drive to a mansion that dwarfed every dwelling Lou had ever seen. The victoria arrived, and she was led between shiny white columns that bordered a wide portico. Once inside, she beheld luxury so extreme, it boggled her. Plush carpet, oak paneling, brass and gold and silver enough to dazzle the eyes. It was, indeed, a whole new realm, as alien as a foreign country.

A butler admitted them. Two maids appeared to take their coats. Festerman dismissed Stephanie and the bodyguards, all except for Vance, who trailed them down a wide hall to a spacious study. Vance stayed in the hall.

In a fireplace crackled a small fire. All four walls were lined with books from floor to ceiling. "Have a seat, won't you?" Festerman requested.

Lou reluctantly obliged. She was biding her time, awaiting a chance to bolt.

"Would you care for a drink?"

"No. I'm not fond of liquor." Inspiration made Lou change her mind. "On second thought, maybe I would." She was hoping he would leave to get it, but she should have known better.

"Vance," Festerman called out. "Have Jarvis bring my usual, plus a gin for the lady." He walked to the divan. "I didn't think to ask. Are you hungry?"

Lou was famished, but she wasn't about to tell him. She didn't want to be beholden to him in any respect. "All I want is to go."

"My answer is still the same." Festerman clasped his hands behind his back and openly ogled her. "You really are quite gorgeous. Your youth, your innocence, they add to your allure."

"I'll bet you say that to all the girls you force into prostitution."

Festerman stepped back in surprise. "How do you—?" he blurted, then pivoted as a commotion broke out in the hall. "Don't move," he said, hurrying to the doorway. Vance and someone else appeared.

Lou couldn't quite see who the second man was, nor could she quite hear what was being said. Once Festerman looked back at her. Or, rather, glowered at her, with an intensity that was frightful to behold.

Lou didn't like it. She gauged the distance to the window and decided she could reach it before they reached her. But to open it, she had to climb on a chair or table, and there were none within quick reach.

"They did what?"

Festerman's growl was like the feral growl of a cougar. Lou began to stand, but he glowered at her again and she sank back down. Another minute of low, excited conversation took place. Then Lon Festerman turned. He was smiling now, but it was a chilling smile, an inhuman smile, the baring of teeth before an attack.

As he turned, Lou saw who was with Vance. Recognition sent a jolt through her. It was Horace, the van driver who had been at Sylvia Banner's. Festerman slammed the door shut behind him and stalked slowly toward her.

"Well, well, well. The outworking of fate never ceases to amaze me. Here you are, my dear, delivered on a silver platter, as it were, saving me the trouble of having to hunt you down."

"Why would you want to do that?"

"Don't patronize me, girl," Festerman said gruffly. "I know all about your little escapade this evening. You and that filthy 'breed fiancé of yours."

Lou shot upright, a retort on the tip of her tongue. A retort she never uttered. For in a rush Lon Festerman reached her and lashed out, knocking her onto the divan.

"You miserable slut!"

A fist was brandished in Lou's face. She could feel blood trickling from the corner of her mouth, and her cheek throbbed.

"So much for wooing you gradually," Festerman said. "So much for a week or two of dining and the theater. There will be no Saturdays at the horse races, no short riverboat trips, no walking along the Mississippi under a full moon."

Lou sat up, braced in case he tried to hit her again, but his initial rage was spent.

Festerman moved toward the fireplace, speaking more to himself than to her. "I was going to go easy on you. I was going to treat you special. And after we made love, if you pleased me, I was going to set you up in your own apartment and arrange for all your expenses to be met."

"I would slit my own throat before I would let you foul me with your touch," Lou told him.

Festerman uttered a wicked laugh. "Listen to her. The bitch still thinks she has a say in the matter." Squatting, he took the poker and thrust it into the flames. "You remind me of someone, Louisa May Clark. Someone who was once very near and dear to me. But like you, she thought she knew better than me. Like you, she bucked me. And, like you, she paid a terrible price for her folly."

"Was it another poor girl you lured off the streets?"

Whirling, Festerman advanced, still clutching the long metal poker. Wisps of smoke rose from the barbed black tip. "No. It was my *daughter*, Mary. She took up with someone below her station, just as you've done. A worthless dirt farmer. I tried to reason with her. I tried to show her that no good would come out of it, that he wasn't fit to wash her feet, let alone marry her, but she refused to listen."

"Where is she now?" Lou nervously asked. His eyes were twin infernos, blazing with madness.

Festerman paused and shook like a leaf in a gale. "She's dead," he said quietly.

"I'm sorry."

"Not as sorry as you will be," Lon Festerman hissed. Elevating the poker, he howled like a wolf gone berserk and charged her.

Chapter Twelve

"You're not happy they helped you?" Zachary King asked. He posed the question as much to take his mind off his worry over Lou as out of curiosity over why Adam Tyler was so upset other gamblers had backed him in the Scarlet Lady. As they were leaving, Tyler had glanced at Worthington's riddled body and remarked, "Damn LeBeau and Carson! They shouldn't have!"

Now, in a carriage speeding toward an address Tyler had given the driver, Zach wanted to know the reason.

"I don't want anyone killed on my account," the man in black responded. "They think that by helping out as they did, no one can pin the blame on me. But Worthington's father might see fit to question everyone who was there and have a list drawn up of all the gamblers who put a slug into his son. Then he'll put a price on our heads."

"You don't know that for sure," Zach pointed out. "You should be glad you have a friends like that big Frenchman."

"Henri *is* one of a kind," Tyler said. "Loyal to a fault."

Zach glanced out the carriage as it took a turn too fast and swayed. "Where are we headed?"

"Lon Festerman's mansion. I told the driver there's twenty dollars in it for him if he gets us there in half the time it usually takes."

"Do you think Festerman will turn Lou over to us without a fight?" Zach didn't care much one way or the other. He'd just as soon take Festerman's scalp.

"The only way he'll let us have her is over his dead body." Tyler looked at him. "I have a favor to ask of you, son."

Zach guessed what it was. "I'm not making any promises. Whoever sees Festerman first kills him first."

"But I'm the one who has a long-standing score to settle," Tyler said. "Thanks to him, the woman I loved was taken from me. My future, my whole life, was ruined. I have more of a right than you do."

"Maybe," Zach acknowledged. "But Lou is *my* fiancée. If I run into him before you do, I'm not going to spare him just so you can satisfy your honor."

"Every man for himself, eh?" Tyler nodded. "Very well. But there will be plenty to go around. He won't be alone. He has a small army of cutthroats at his disposal. I can't predict how many will be at his estate, but it's bound to be well-guarded."

As they soon confirmed. Tyler had directed the driver to stop a quarter of a mile from the mansion. They went the rest of the way on foot to avoid being noticed. Soon they came to a high wall that surrounded the property and glided soundlessly along its base until they drew within sight of an ornate gate.

Zach grabbed the gambler's sleeve and stopped. "Look!" he whispered. "In the shadows." He had spied two men holding shotguns.

"How on earth did you spot them?"

For someone who had spent his whole life in the wilderness, it came as naturally as breathing. All of Zach's senses had been honed by the daily pressures of living in the wild. Those who survived were those who stayed alert. For any man or animal to lower their guard for even a moment was to court oblivion.

"One of them moved," Zach said, and let it go at that.

Backing off a dozen yards, they faced the wall. "I'll give you a boost, then you help me," Tyler proposed, cupping his hands.

Zach slid his right foot onto the gambler's linked palms, tensed, and vaulted up. At the selfsame instant, the man in black levered his arms and shoulders. Like an oversized bird, Zach sailed to the top and seized hold. Lying on his stomach, he reached down. "Jump."

Tyler backed up a few feet, took a running start, and pumped upward. His fingers snagged Zach's. Zach was able to hold on, but the sudden weight caused him to shift and he nearly lost his balance. Locking his legs, he anchored himself. Tyler swiftly climbed up beside him.

Dropping lightly to the other side, they glided toward the mansion. The acreage around it was preserved in a pristine state, with lush gardens and countless maples and oaks.

It was almost like being in a forest. Zach felt right at home. Ahead were lilacs, which he skirted. Then he dropped into a crouch and froze at the sight of a lanky figure coming toward them. He slid his hand under his shirt to the extra weapon he had brought.

Tyler's right arm flicked, and his derringer flashed dully in the night.

"No," Zach whispered. "We can't make any noise."

"Then how—?" Tyler asked, but Zach was already moving, sliding on his hands and knees to an oak ten feet away. He slowly rose, the Bowie at his side, then eased his right eye around the trunk far enough to see.

The man carried a shotgun, and he wasn't alone. At the end of a short leash strained a huge dog, a black brute with long legs and a short tail.

Zach didn't know what kind it was, but it was trouble. Its ears were pricked toward the lilacs and it was panting and whining, anxious to be let loose. He couldn't possibly kill both the sentry and the dog without one or the other making some sort of sound that would bring others on the run.

They halted, and the man brought the shotgun up.

Zach glanced at the lilacs and couldn't believe what he was seeing. Adam Tyler had strolled into the open, his hands shoved into his pockets. Whistling as if he didn't have a care in the world, his head bent low.

"Hold it right there, mister!"

Tyler raised his head. "What's wrong? Mr. Festerman assured me it was all right to take a stroll."

"You know him?" the sentry asked suspiciously. The black dog was rumbling deep in its chest, spoiling to attack if given the command.

"We played cards all evening at the Scarlet Lady," Tyler lied. "Surely you saw me get out of his carriage?"

"I didn't pay much attention," the man said. He was approximately eight feet from the oak, standing side-on to the trunk. "But it's not like him to give visitors the run of the grounds at this time of night. You'll have to come with me so I can verify your story."

"Whatever you want," Tyler said. "Just keep that beast of yours under control. I don't want to be bitten." Tyler angled toward the mansion, giving the cutthroat and his dog a wide berth.

The man rotated, keeping Tyler in front of him, which put the man's back to the tree—and to Zach. Two long bounds, and Zach slid ten inches of cold steel slid between the sentry's ribs, piercing his heart. Dead before he knew he had been stabbed, the man crumbled. Zach barely broke stride, and yanking the blade out, he sprang at the dog, which had heard him and was swiveling.

A sliver of silver flashed. The dog yipped once as the hilt of a dagger sprouted in its side. Then it did as its master had done and lay twitching.

Adam Tyler reclaimed his dagger and wiped it clean on the watchdog's pelt. He fitted the dagger up his left sleeve in a special rig much like the one that held his derringer up his right sleeve. "Let's hope no one heard," he said softly.

Side by side they jogged on. They were a stone's throw from the mansion when they spied another guard standing beside a gazebo, smoking a cigarette. Veering to the right, they avoided him and presently were crossing a final belt of cropped grass.

Zach slid the Bowie under his belt and drew both pistols. The windows were low enough to the ground that he could peer in, and he went from one to another, seeking sign of his betrothed. He was almost to the rear when he glanced back and was startled to discover Adam Tyler had disappeared.

Reversing direction, Zach came to a darkened window that had been opened. The gambler was inside! Tyler had gone after Lon Festerman on his own. Furious, Zach wasted no time climbing in. He fretted that Tyler's thirst for vengeance would endanger Lou.

Zach was in a long room. A door cracked open at the other end admitted enough light to serve as a beacon. He moved rapidly, gritting his teeth when he bumped his knee on a chair. At the doorway he paused to listen and heard nothing out of the ordinary. Cautiously pushing the door wider, he checked in both directions. To the right the hallway was empty, but to the left he glimpsed Adam Tyler slipping into another room farther down. He stepped out to follow, then immediately drew back. Beyond Tyler were two other men, one of whom was vaguely familiar.

A second after Zach realized where he had seen the man before, the house pealed to a high-pitched scream.

Louisa couldn't help herself. She'd always considered it weak of grown women to scream in a crisis, but as Lon Festerman leaped toward her with the hot poker raised to bash in her skull, she instinctively shrieked.

158

With an audible swish, the poker cleaved the air. Lou rolled to the right and heard it thud into the divan. Falling onto the floor, she continued to roll. A thunk behind her testified to how close Festerman had come to spearing her a second time.

"Damned bitch!"

Lou came to a stop on her hands and knees. Festerman wasn't giving her a moment's respite. He was on her again, swinging wildly. She ducked under the first blow, then skittered to the left and shoved upright. The dress hampered her, its folds clinging to her legs, restricting her movements.

"You're mine!" Festerman raged, lancing the poker at her abdomen.

Not if Lou could help it. She flung herself backward, then pivoted, seeking to get past him and reach the door. Although what benefit that would be with Vance and Horace out in the hall remained to be seen. She only knew she had to distance herself from the poker, whatever it took.

Lon Festerman slowed, a cruel smear of a smile creasing his thin mouth. "Go ahead. Make it harder for me. I'll enjoy it that much more."

The echoes of the scream hadn't faded when Zach stepped into the hallway and brought up his pistols. But before he could fire, Adam Tyler slid from the other room and rushed toward the driver of the van and a burly man, both of whom had their ears pressed to yet a third door.

Zach pegged it as the room Lou was in. He flew down the hall, his heart racing faster than his feet. *Festerman must be trying to force himself on her!* Zach suspected, and had a burning urge to put a lead ball between the bastard's eyes.

Horace heard Adam Tyler bearing down and straightened. He shouted a warning as he clawed for a pistol, but he had not yet cleared his jacket when the gambler's derringer spat flame and smoke. Horace staggered, his left eye gone, and as he oozed to the floor the other man came to life, drawing a short-barreled flintlock.

Again the gambler's derringer cracked and the second man shared Horace's fate. Tyler cleared both their bodies and was through the door in a blur.

Shouts and bellows were breaking out all over the place. Zach reached the two dead men and shoved against the door, only to find that for some reason it wouldn't budge. It was either locked or blocked.

"Lou!" he cried.

A door down the hall opened. A man and a woman in black and white outfits rushed out but retreated when Zach showed his pistols.

"Lou! Tyler! Open the door!"

Zach could hear voices on the other side, but he couldn't make out what was being said. He rammed his shoulder against the panel, but it resisted. About to try again, he swung around at a resounding crash.

The front door had been flung open. Into the mansion hurtled two thugs with shotguns.

Lon Festerman was trying to drive Lou into a corner. He speared the poker to one side, then the other, forcing her to retreat. Two shots in the hallway brought him up short, and they both glanced at the door as it was pushed open and slammed shut again by a tall man in a black frock coat and wide black hat. Lou assumed he was one of Festerman's underlings, but Festerman seemed shocked.

"You!"

The tall man grabbed a chair and braced it against the door so no one else could get in. Then he turned. "Here I thought you might have forgotten me," he said with a sneer.

"Forget the worthless son of a bitch who took my daughter from me?" Festerman responded. "I've dreamt of this day! But I never really believed you would dare show your miserable face, Vaughn!"

Lou saw the man raise a smoking derringer. "I changed my name years ago. It's Tyler now. Adam Tyler."

"The gambler I've heard so much about?" Festerman said in surprise. "You've been in St. Louis all this time and you've never looked me up?"

"I was waiting for a formal invitation," Tyler taunted.

"Go ahead, then! Shoot, since you're not man enough to confront me without a gun."

"It's empty." Tyler pocketed the derringer and moved forward. "It will be you and me. Man to man. More fitting that way, don't you agree?"

Lon Festerman moved to meet the man in black halfway. "I hope Mary is watching from on high. I want her to see me send you to hell."

Zach snapped off a shot that caught one of the guards in the chest and twirled him around. As the man keeled over, the second cutthroat let loose with his shotgun. At that range it would have blown Zach in half, only Zach flattened. Lethal hornets buzzed overhead as he fired the other pistol. The second guard lost part of his head in a shower of gore and hair.

Pushing onto his knees, Zach turned to the pair Tyler had shot. He appropriated Horace's flintlock and the short-barreled pistol.

On the other side of the door someone was yelling.

"Lou!" Zach tried again. "Let me in!" He rose to renew his assault on the panel, but just then heavy feet pounded on a flight of stairs midway down the hall. Two more of Festerman's thugs were descending, one with a pistol, the other with a rifle. Zach saw them before they saw him. Taking deliberate aim, he felled the first man. The second got off a shot, the slug digging into the wall beside Zach's ear. Zach returned fire, the short-barreled pistol booming loud. The would-be killer grabbed at his shattered face and pitched forward.

Zach couldn't reload. He had no ammunition. Running to the fallen duo by the front door, he retrieved a shotgun. No sooner had he done so than another guard filled the entrance. The man was a shade slow in reacting and paid for it with his life.

Out front more of Festerman's hardcases were yelling back and forth. Zach peered out and saw half a dozen converging from different directions. Helping himself to another shotgun, he stayed by the door, determined to make a stand and drive them off or die in the attempt.

Lou heard someone shout, out in the hallway. She was aware of a thud on the door and a series of shots. But she was too mesmerized by the fight unfolding in front of her to pay much attention.

Adam Tyler had met Lon Festerman in the center of the study. From out of thin air the tall man in black pulled a dagger, which he wielded with exceptional skill, parrying the poker again and again, slashing when an opening presented itself. Lon Festerman thrust, swung, stabbed, and clubbed, growing more and more frantic as the seconds ticked by.

The dagger opened two wounds, a cut high on Festerman's right shoulder and another low across his ribs. Neither was serious, but blood was flowing and they had to hurt. Festerman didn't seem to care. He drove the poker at Tyler's throat, and when the tall man countered, Festerman shifted and sheared the tip at his foe's thigh.

Tyler sidestepped, but not quite quickly enough. The poker tore through his pants and dug a deep furrow. Wincing, Tyler skipped back.

Festerman slowly circled, wagging the poker's bloody point in small circles. "That's just for starters. I want you to suffer for the torment you caused me. To suffer as no one has ever suffered before."

"Don't you dare preach to me about torment," Adam Tyler said. "There isn't a day that goes by I don't feel like ending it, just to be with her again. She was everything to me. Everything! And your assassins murdered her."

"You blame me?" Festerman said bitterly. "Mary would still be alive today if you had done as I wanted and left her alone. But no! You snuck around behind my back. You schemed to elope." Festerman feinted, and when the man

162

in black dodged, he continued to circle. "You couldn't leave well enough alone."

"And you couldn't bear the idea of Mary having a life of her own. You had to control her, just like you control everyone else."

"I loved her!" Festerman roared, then flailed the poker as if it were a club.

Lou saw Tyler withstand a flurry that would have brought most men to their knees. Suddenly the dagger streaked out and in. Festerman, slashed across the back of his right wrist, danced out of harm's way.

More shots in the hall heightened the tension. Festerman cocked his head. "So you brought help? Not that anyone can save you. You're not leaving this room alive."

Tyler glanced at Lou. "Your fiancé is out there. Go to him."

"Zach?" Lou dashed toward the door, but Lon Festerman was in her way and he renewed his fierce attempt to batter the tall man into the floor. Swinging without letup, he unleashed his most devastating attack yet.

Lou darted to the left so she wouldn't be hit. Suddenly a tremendous blast at the front of the mansion made her think a score of cannons had discharged a ragged volley. Lou's hand rose to her throat. Her beloved was in a battle for his life!

The half-dozen guards were crossing the grass strip when Zach stepped into the entrance and triggered a shotgun blast that bowled one over. He ducked behind the jamb as five shotguns thundered in kind.

Out on the lawn a man groaned. Another hollered for everyone to rush the mansion at once.

Zach had used the last of the available guns. The cut-throats would overwhelm him and slay Adam Tyler and Lou unless he thought of something—and thought of it right away. Cupping a hand to his mouth, Zach called out, "Get killed for nothing if that's what you want! The man who hired you is dead!"

163

Silence ensued for all of thirty seconds. "How do we know you're not lying?" someone finally replied.

"Didn't you hear all the shots in here?" Zach rejoined. As a Shoshone warrior, it went against his grain to resort to trickery rather than to defeat an adversary in combat. But he excused his ruse with the thought that Lou was worth more than his honor. "Festerman was the first to fall."

"We want to see his body!" a different thug demanded.

"Come right on in, then!" Zach said. "We'll be more than happy to have you join him! All of you!"

They commenced talking among themselves, shouting back and forth.

"Do you think he's telling the truth?" one asked.

"There was an awful lot of shooting," someone else noted.

"How'd they get past us and reach the mansion?" was another's main concern.

"Who the hell cares? They did, and now we're likely out of work. Hell, we knew something like this would happen one day. The boss had more enemies than I have hairs on my head."

"So what do we do?"

"I don't know about the rest of you, but I'm not dying for a dead man."

Zach waited in breathless anticipation, but no one else spoke. After a bit he risked taking a peek and spotted a knot of men fleeing down the drive toward the gate. They had decided living was the better part of valor. Spinning, he ran down the hall. This time the door wouldn't keep him out!

Adam Tyler had retreated as far as he could go. His back was to the wall. Lon Festerman had him trapped, and they both knew it. Beaming, Festerman bent at the knees and stabbed at his stomach, but the poker missed, sinking into the wood instead.

"This is for Mary," Tyler said, cleaving the double-edged dagger upward. It sliced into Festerman's jaw, splitting flesh like an overripe fruit.

Swearing luridly, pumping scarlet, Festerman jumped backward. Stumbling, he sank onto a knee.

"This is for the family Mary and I never had." Adam Tyler hewed the dagger into Lon's upper arm. Festerman sought to retaliate, but his muscles had been severed.

"This is for the happiness you deprived us of."

Lou had started toward the door, but she couldn't tear her eyes from the tall man's vengeance. It was awful to behold.

"This is for all the other lives you've ruined."

Lon Festerman was covered with blood and swaying as if drunk, his arms limp at his sides. "Damn you," he said weakly.

The man in black raised the dagger one last time. "And this is what I should have done the night Mary died. What I've wanted to do every night ever since. What you deserve." Bending, Tyler buried the dagger in Festerman's groin. Then, gripping the hilt with both hands, he sheared upward.

Lou had to turn away or be ill. She jumped when the door abruptly crashed inward and into the study spilled a young dark-haired man in fine city-bought clothes. It took a moment for her to recognize who it was. "Zach?" Lou cried, flinging herself at him.

"Lou?" Zachary King embraced his sweetheart, hugging her trembling form close. He never wanted to let her go. "I thought I'd lost you." Zach would have been perfectly happy to stand there forever, but his gaze drifted to what was left of the scourge of St. Louis, reminding him they weren't out of danger yet. "We have to light a shuck," he said. "More of Festerman's men might show up."

Adam Tyler had risen. "We'll go over the back wall. You can stay at my place tonight, with Milhouse. Tomorrow we'll pay Sylvia Banner a visit and persuade her there are healthier climates elsewhere."

Zach verified that the hallway was empty. From the study he led them to the dark room and out the window. He'd never seen Lou in a dress before and couldn't get over how lovely she was. It made him all the more eager to be alone with her, to show exactly how much he had missed her.

"Is it really over?" Louisa marveled as they plunged into a maple grove.

"In more ways than one," the man in black said.

No one challenged them. No one opened fire. Ten minutes later, they had scaled the wall and were searching for an empty carriage to hail.

Louisa May Clark nestled her cheek against Zach's shoulder and smiled. Now they could hunt up her relatives. In a month or so they would head back to the Rockies, and shortly after that they would be united as man and wife. Her dream was coming true.

Zach glanced at Tyler. "I'll never be able to thank you enough. What will you do now that Festerman is dead?"

The gambler thought a moment. "I think I'll learn how to live again."

WILDERNESS

#24

Mountain Madness

←——————————→

David Thompson

When Nate King comes upon a pair of green would-be trappers from New York, he is only too glad to risk his life to save them from a Piegan war party. It is only after he takes them into his own cabin that he realizes they will repay his kindness...with betrayal. When the backshooters reveal their true colors, Nate knows he is in for a brutal battle—with the lives of his family hanging in the balance.

___4399-8 $3.99 US/$4.99 CAN

Dorchester Publishing Co., Inc.
P.O. Box 6640
Wayne, PA 19087-8640

WILDERNESS

#25
FRONTIER MAYHEM

$\longleftrightarrow$

David Thompson

The unforgiving wilderness of the Rocky Mountains forces a boy to grow up fast, so Nate King taught his son, Zach, how to survive the constant hazards and hardships—and he taught him well. With an Indian war party on the prowl and a marauding grizzly on the loose, young Zach is about to face the test of his life, with no room for failure. But there is one danger Nate hasn't prepared Zach for—a beautiful girl with blue eyes.

___4433-1 $3.99 US/$4.99 CAN

Dorchester Publishing Co., Inc.
P.O. Box 6640
Wayne, PA 19087-8640

Please add $1.75 for shipping and handling for the first book and $.50 for each book thereafter. NY, NYC, and PA residents, please add appropriate sales tax. No cash, stamps, or C.O.D.s. All orders shipped within 6 weeks via postal service book rate. Canadian orders require $2.00 extra postage and must be paid in U.S. dollars through a U.S. banking facility.

Name_____
Address_____
City_____State_____Zip_____
I have enclosed $_____ in payment for the checked book(s).
Payment <u>must</u> accompany all orders. ❑ Please send a free catalog.
    CHECK OUT OUR WEBSITE! www.dorchesterpub.com

WILDERNESS

BLOOD FEUD

David Thompson

The brutal wilderness of the Rocky Mountains can be deadly to those unaccustomed to its dangers. So when a clan of travelers from the hill country back East arrive at Nate King's part of the mountain, Nate is more than willing to lend a hand and show them some hospitality. He has no way of knowing that this clan is used to fighting—and killing—for what they want. And they want Nate's land for their own!

___4477-3 $3.99 US/$4.99 CAN

WILDERNESS

#27
GOLD RAGE

DAVID THOMPSON

Penniless old trapper Ben Frazier is just about ready to pack it all in when an Arapaho warrior takes pity on him and shows him where to find the elusive gold that white men value so greatly. His problems seem to be over, but then another band of trappers finds out about the gold and forces Ben to lead them to it. It's up to Zach King to save the old man, but can he survive a fight against a gang of gold-crazed mountain men?

___4519-2 $3.99 US/$4.99 CAN

Dorchester Publishing Co., Inc.
P.O. Box 6640
Wayne, PA 19087-8640

Please add $1.75 for shipping and handling for the first book and $.50 for each book thereafter. NY, NYC, and PA residents, please add appropriate sales tax. No cash, stamps, or C.O.D.s. All orders shipped within 6 weeks via postal service book rate. Canadian orders require $2.00 extra postage and must be paid in U.S. dollars through a U.S. banking facility.

Name_____
Address_____
City_____State_____Zip_____
I have enclosed $_____ in payment for the checked book(s).
Payment <u>must</u> accompany all orders. ❑ Please send a free catalog.
CHECK OUT OUR WEBSITE! www.dorchesterpub.com

WILDERNESS

TRAPPER'S BLOOD/
MOUNTAIN CAT

DAVID THOMPSON

Trapper's Blood. In the wild Rockies, a man has to act as judge, jury, and executioner against his enemies. And when trappers start turning up dead, their bodies horribly mutilated, Nate King and his friends vow to hunt down the ruthless killers. But taking the law into their own hands, they soon find out that a hasty decision can make them as guilty as the murderers they want to stop.

And in the same action-packed volume…

Mountain Cat. A seasoned hunter and trapper, Nate King can fend off attacks from brutal warriors and furious grizzlies alike. But a hunt for a mountain lion twice the size of other deadly cats proves to be his greatest challenge. If Nate can't destroy the monstrous creature, it will slaughter innocent settlers—and the massacre might well begin with Nate's own family!

___4621-0 $4.99 US/$5.99 CAN

Dorchester Publishing Co., Inc.
P.O. Box 6640
Wayne, PA 19087-8640

Please add $1.75 for shipping and handling for the first book and $.50 for each book thereafter. NY, NYC, and PA residents, please add appropriate sales tax. No cash, stamps, or C.O.D.s. All orders shipped within 6 weeks via postal service book rate. Canadian orders require $2.00 extra postage and must be paid in U.S. dollars through a U.S. banking facility.

Name_____
Address_____
City_____State_____Zip_____
I have enclosed $_____ in payment for the checked book(s).
Payment <u>must</u> accompany all orders. ❑ Please send a free catalog.
CHECK OUT OUR WEBSITE! www.dorchesterpub.com

WILDERNESS DOUBLE EDITION

DAVID THOMPSON

MOUNTAIN DEVIL/ BLACKFOOT MASSACRE

The epic struggle for survival in America's untamed West.

Mountain Devil. In 1832, when Nate leads a hunting expedition into a valley where Indian legend says one of the fiercest creatures lives, he might become the prey of a beast that has come out of his worst nightmare.

And in the same action-packed volume...

Blackfoot Massacre. When the Reverend John Burke is trapped in perilous Blackfoot territory, Nate has to save the man—or he'll bear the brand of a coward until the day he dies.

___4327-0 $4.99 US/$5.99 CAN

Dorchester Publishing Co., Inc.
P.O. Box 6640
Wayne, PA 19087-8640

WILDERNESS

WINTERKILL/ BLOOD TRUCE

⬅➡

David Thompson

Winterkill. The unexplored Rockies hide threats that can kill even the most experienced mountain men. But when Nathaniel King takes in a pair of strangers who have lost their way in the snow, his kindness is repaid with vile treachery. If King isn't careful, he and his young family will not live to see another spring.

And in the same action-packed volume...

Blood Truce. With only raw courage to aid them, Nate King and other pioneers brave the constant threat of Indian attack to claim the freedom they find on the frontier. But when a deadly dispute among rival tribes blows up into a bloody war, Nate has to make peace between the enemies—or he and his family will be the first to lose their scalps.

___4489-7 $4.99 US/$5.99 CAN

WILDERNESS DOUBLE EDITION

SAVE $$$!

Savage Rendezvous by David Thompson. In 1828, the Rocky Mountains are an immense, unsettled region through which few white men dare travel. Only courageous mountain men like Nathaniel King are willing to risk the unknown dangers for the freedom the wilderness offers. But while attending a rendezvous of trappers and fur traders, King's freedom is threatened when he is accused of murdering several men for their money. With the help of his friend Shakespeare McNair, Nate has to prove his innocence. For he has not cast off the fetters of society to spend the rest of his life behind bars.

And in the same action-packed volume...

Blood Fury by David Thompson. On a hunting trip, young Nathaniel King stumbles onto a disgraced Crow Indian. Attempting to regain his honor, Sitting Bear places himself and his family in great peril, for a war party of hostile Utes threatens to kill them all. When the savages wound Sitting Bear and kidnap his wife and daughter, Nathaniel has to rescue them or watch them perish. But despite his skill in tricking unfriendly Indians, King may have met an enemy he cannot outsmart.

__4208-8 $4.99 US/$5.99 CAN

Dorchester Publishing Co., Inc.
P.O. Box 6640
Wayne, PA 19087-8640

Please add $1.75 for shipping and handling for the first book and $.50 for each book thereafter. NY, NYC, and PA residents, please add appropriate sales tax. No cash, stamps, or C.O.D.s. All orders shipped within 6 weeks via postal service book rate. Canadian orders require $2.00 extra postage and must be paid in U.S. dollars through a U.S. banking facility.

Name_____
Address_____
City_____ State_____ Zip_____
I have enclosed $_____ in payment for the checked book(s).
Payment <u>must</u> accompany all orders. ☐ Please send a free catalog.